HONOR RESPECT
DEVOTION
A NOVELLA

LINDA K. RODANTE
CONTEMPORARY CHRISTIAN ROMANCE WITH SUSPENSE

Lone Mesa Publishing

www.lonemesapublishing.com
Honor Respect Devotion
ISBN 978-1-947869-81-3
Copyright © 2016 Linda K. Rodante

Special Thanks!

To my Tarpon Writer's group, my Word Weavers Tampa group, to my beta readers, and reviewers! Thank you all for so much help and input.

Thanks especially to MaryLou Hess and Rebecca Zuch who allow me to pick their brains one-on-one when I need to.

Thanks to Teri Burns for a great cover, for formatting and uploading, and doing all the techy stuff for me! Lone Mesa Publishing, you rock!

Thanks, also, to the Christian Indie Author Group and the Clean Indie Reads group on Facebook for their quick answers to many questions.

Special thanks to my nephew, Wes Knadle, Aviation Maintenance Technician with the U.S. Coast Guard, for answering my questions and giving me needed input for this book.*

And a heartfelt thanks to all the men and women of the U.S. Coast Guard for the wonderful job they do in saving lives during dangerous times.

As always, thanks to my husband and my family for their faith in me and their encouragement.

If not for God the Father, and the Lord Jesus Christ, none of this would ever get done. I thank and praise Him that in the midst of life's severe ups and downs, He can take us to a place of rest and peace and love.

❧

All characters and events in this book are fictional. Any problem with Coast Guard procedures or actions is solely that of the author, either for fictional purposes or because she misunderstood information given to her.

❧

Pornography is a hard subject. It entraps and enslaves, and causes others to be entrapped and enslaved to satisfy another person's sexual addiction. Internet pornography is often hidden and can lead to physical (ED) and emotional and marital problems. Porn is cited as a contributing reason for divorce in 56% of cases.

** Furthermore, 88% of pornographic films show acts of violence or physical aggression toward women and children.**

To learn more about pornography and how to help yourself, a loved one, or friend get free from this addiction, check out www.covenanteyes.com or http://endsexualexploitation.org/

**The Porn Circuit: Understand Your Brain and Break Porn Habits in 90 Days*, by Covenant Eyes, 2013. Or go to www.covenanteyes.com/science-of-porn-addiction-ebook

Prologue

"Mark. Nine o'clock. Mark. Nine o'clock." The flight mechanic's voice jumped at Jake Travis Osborne. "Two people in the water. Two survivors at nine o'clock."

Jake brought the MH-60 Jayhawk US Coast Guard helicopter around and cast a glance at the Gulf waters below. The orange life preservers stood out. The pair held on to each other or, more likely, had tied themselves together. Kudos to whoever thought of that.

"Forward and right 60." The flight mechanic's voice leapt again.

Jake adjusted the cyclic stick. Below them, the helicopter's blades created a cracked-glass surface on the Gulf of Mexico. What Jake couldn't see, but knew was happening, was that a man and his preteen daughter—if their briefing was correct—were getting hammered by frothy seas from winds kicked up by those same blades.

"Forward and right 40."

Jake made the adjustment. The whump-whump of the propeller echoed in his ears.

"Checklist complete. Ready for deployment of rescue swimmer." The voice paused, then continued. "Rescue swimmer out the door. Swimmer going down."

Jake kept his attention on the flight controls but never stopped listening to the checklist litany.

"Swimmer's away. Swimmer's okay."

Rescue swimmer Zeke Thompson would keep his distance from the pair below until the basket was lowered. He'd calm them with a joke, probably ask who ordered pizza, and then judge the level of medical need.

The two had survived the April night, but even in summer weather, the Gulf of Mexico could produce hypothermia—a real threat, along with their exhaustion.

"Swimmer's calling for the basket.

"Trail line is connected. Basket is out the door.

"Back. Left 10.

"Hold. Hold."

"Bringing survivor up."

The silence stretched, then, "Survivor below cabin door." Another long pause followed by the shape and shift of the basket coming on board. "Hoist complete."

A collective release of tension filled the helicopter's interior, but only for a moment. Jake listened as his mechanic/lifter/medic moved the survivor, most likely the girl, from the basket to the fold-down chair against the helo's inside wall. The crew would check her medically, make sure she was stable, then send the basket down again.

"Basket's going out the door.

"Basket's in the water.

"Forward and right 60. Hold.

"Second survivor's in..." The litany stopped. A long pause followed.

Holding tight to the stick, Jake glanced at his copilot. Charley Ford raised an eyebrow, looked over his shoulder, then shook his head.

"Survivor's arm is broken." The tone of the mechanic's voice changed. "Zeke's having some trouble with him. Hold her steady."

Jake's jaw clenched. With the helo's wash pounding them and the seas slapping their faces, they didn't need any more trouble down there. He forced his concentration to the stick and prayed.

They were not going to lose this man. He'd joined the Coast Guard for this purpose—that he'd be part of saving those who needed saving. *To save all.* Not just some.

The hard punch of the waves and the taste of salt filled his mind. He knew what Zeke and the man were going through. He knew what the girl had just survived. He'd been there himself. A day and a night that he tried not to remember. His chest tightened.

Come on, Lord. Help Zeke. The girl needs her father.

"Back, left 30."

Jake adjusted the stick and continued his silent prayer. Behind him, the girl's voice rose in a frantic plea for her dad. His copilot unhooked himself and slipped into the back.

"Hold! Hold!" The flight mechanic's voice cut across the girl's.

Jake tightened his grip. He couldn't see what was going on below. He held to blind faith in his crew. The whop-whop of the blades sounded louder. The muscles across his shoulders tightened.

Okay, Lord. Blind faith in you.

"Survivor's in basket." The flight mechanic's words cracked the thick atmosphere. "Survivor's on the way up."

The copilot's voice as he comforted the daughter slid like warm oil to Jake's ears. Still, he waited.

"Basket in position." A beat passed, two, then three. "Basket's in the cabin."

Jake grinned. *Thank you, Lord.* He welcomed the noises from the back—the team lifting the man from the basket, the man's groan of pain, and the girl's relieved sobbing. The two were on board and safe.

"Getting rescue swimmer." Another pause.

"Swimmer coming up."

"Swimmer's inside."

"Cabin door closed."

"Ready for forward flight."

Charley climbed into his seat. His grin echoed Jake's. "Another story for that news lady who's been

hounding us. Head for home, J.T. I'll radio for an
ambulance to meet us."

The words caused a surge of adrenaline. Relief
swirled inside Jake. The other victory in his life mixed
with it. A victory that was three years old, but the
freedom he felt because of it never ceased to amaze him.

He swung the helo around and headed for
Clearwater.

Chapter 1

China Summers shifted to see the rearview mirror. The shoulder-length black hair looked natural, almost the same as her hair had looked two and a half years ago. She nodded, slid from behind the wheel of her small sports car, and stared at the church. She'd changed, feeling more like thirty than twenty-one. Would anyone believe it? Names and faces ran through her mind. Maybe. Maybe one.

She'd never pegged herself as a coward, so she lifted her head, tossed the uncertainty aside, and strode toward the front doors. God had a reason for leading her back here. Too bad He hadn't told her what it was.

Towering heels, tight white shirt, and short black skirt perhaps hadn't been the best choices today. Leftovers from that previous life. Knowing what to do and doing it was still a struggle, but one she'd win—with God's help.

She hesitated before pulling the door open. Maybe he was here after all. She smiled, but only for a minute. He might welcome her back, but his wife wouldn't.

Jake Osborne came from the youth room after the last of the teenagers exited. The morning Bible study had faced a challenge—Eric Johnson questioning Jake's interpretation of the Scriptures they were studying. The teen had not asked a serious question but had tried to throw the whole discussion into turmoil. With the type of life Jake lived, it would take more than an Eric Johnson to rattle him.

He slipped his phone into his pocket and started

up the aisle toward the back of the church. His comfort level as part of the church still amazed him. The dramatic change in his life three years ago *today* had altered his attitude and relationships—for the good. People walked toward him, filling the chairs on either side. He returned the smiles and the greetings before shifting his gaze to the back doors.

When they swung inward this time, he stopped. A girl he didn't recognize stepped through. Raven hair swung just below her shoulders, deep-red lipstick highlighted porcelain pale skin, and the shortest skirt he'd seen in a long time hugged her hips. A tattoo on her right thigh peeked from beneath the skirt. He jerked in recognition. His gaze flew back to her face. No. A different face, but the tattoo and its placement…

Her glance slid around the room and fastened on him. She met his look and straightened. Her head tilted. The red lips parted.

Emotion surged through him. He forced his focus to the wall behind her and the picture of Jesus surrounded by children, then whirled and marched back down the aisle.

Rage shot up his spine. How like the enemy to bring someone through the doors today to tear at the victory he'd won. He weaved around the people coming up the aisle, headed to the side door, and almost slammed into the man coming through it.

"Hey." John Jergenson's voice and hand on his arm stopped him. "You running out, Jake?"

"Just need some air."

"You got something against the air in here?"

"Nothing that being outside won't help." Jake threw a glance over his shoulder.

John looked past him, and the amusement dropped from his face. His hand fell from Jake's arm. "China."

❧

China met John's surprised stare. The other man disappeared through the doorway. She took a long breath and questioned herself again. Why hadn't she worn one of the outfits she'd bought for church? Because she didn't want anyone to look too close. Let them stare at the short skirt and the tight shirt.

John walked up the aisle toward her. She wondered how the Christianity they all touted would do today.

"China." His voice sounded the same, the gentle lilt of country overshadowed by whatever accent he'd picked up from an Italian-American dad and a Swedish mom. Gentle, warm, often amused—but not now.

Wary. That was how he sounded. She couldn't blame him.

She smiled. "Hey. How're you doing?"

"We're doing well. Are you home for a visit?"

She heard the plural in his answer and was not surprised. He'd drawn a line quickly. Other people filed past. Some she knew. A few forced a smile and nodded. Others' eyes widened. One or two actually gave real smiles.

"Home, but not home. I've rented a house."

His brows lifted. "A house? You're not with your mom?"

"No. I've been on my own for two years. Didn't feel right moving back."

"You're staying then?"

"Yep. What do you think?"

"I think there's more to it than you're saying."

China straightened. He was the only one who had ever tried to look past the exterior. It used to irritate her. Now, though...

"Babe?"

China turned at the female voice. His wife stood

there—hair as wild as ever, same petite body, the hazel eyes widening in surprise—with a baby cuddled in her arms.

"Hi, Sharee." China forced her own smile. "I'm back."

John slipped an arm around his wife's shoulders. "It's good to have you back, China, but the service is about to start. Let's talk later." He took the baby from Sharee's arms and held him against his shoulder, and they moved down the aisle to their seats.

China watched them slip into their seats before she found one for herself. *Not everyone's glad, that's for sure.* Not Sharee. Not the guy who ran off. A new guy. Not too tall, especially compared with John, but fit, with sandy-blond hair and blue eyes. Must be other new members, too, since she left. She glanced around. Not that she was interested. The last guy in her life had left a mark the size of the Grand Canyon. It had taken a while to heal. In fact, the scars still ran deep.

The band began to play, the worship leader started the first song, and China stood with the rest of the congregation to join in. Words about grace and God's love filled the sanctuary. China closed her eyes. She swallowed and fought against the pain in her throat.

God, I don't know why I'm here. There are thousands of churches in this country. Why here? Wetness formed behind her eyelids. *I can't change the past, even though I wish I could. And the future, Lord, the future doesn't look good at all.*

"Take China Summers with you."

The pastor's voice stopped Jake in his tracks. He glanced over his shoulder, his hand still on the office door. "China?"

"Yes. You haven't met her, but ask Ryann Byrd. She knows her. China used to help with the youth two or three years ago, before you came."

A picture of the young woman in the too-short skirt, sporting the raven tattoo, popped full blown into his mind. He'd never had a problem picturing things. In fact, that was a problem itself. Caution whispered up his spine. He turned. "The girl with the tattoo?"

Pastor Alan tilted his head. "We have quite a few young people with tattoos these days, but I did hear China's name mentioned in particular about that."

"That's understandable."

The pastor said nothing for a moment. "I didn't see you at service yesterday. That must be some gossip grapevine we have if you've heard about it already."

Jake hesitated. He and the pastor had an agreement. Did his reason for leaving Sunday fit into that agreement? "I left before the service started. Sorry. However, the girl's outfit was…extremely suggestive."

Pastor Alan nodded. "That was mentioned to me, but China's back for a reason. I'm not saying anything about that to someone who's maybe looking for help—or at least a friendly face. The Church has done that type of thing too much in the past. Jesus came to save the lost, not kick them out."

Jake nodded. He agreed with the sentiment, but caution still held him immobile.

"Is this a problem, Jake?" The pastor's brows lifted fractionally. "Our agreement still holds, correct?"

"Yes, the agreement holds."

"You have anything to tell me?"

"No."

"Good. Take China and Ryann and check out this park and campground you've been telling me about. I wasn't comfortable with you and Ryann going by yourselves after Matt dropped out. Having another person will make things look better to some of our congregation that worry about that kind of thing." He waved a hand to stop Jake's protest. "If you want to take the youth there, we need the women's opinions anyway. You know that. If they aren't happy, you'll have your hands full."

Jake had planned the day trip to include Ryann and her boyfriend, Matthew, but Matt had called to say he had to work. The trip was an innocent scouting expedition for a weekend retreat, but as a youth pastor, spending the whole day with one of his female helpers might cause some tongues to flap.

He shook his head. Someone had warned him that his work with the Coast Guard would prove easier than being a youth pastor. He hadn't believed them. His mistake.

≈

Saturday at 7:00 AM, Jake sat in his Jeep and watched Ryann and China pull into the church parking lot. The morning air swirled around and past him. Goose bumps rose on his bare arms, but he preferred the cool to the heat. The daytime temps in Florida during April could jump from a mild seventy degrees to a sweaty eighty-five, unlike the water temperature where they were headed. The underground springs feeding the water there kept it at a brisk seventy-two degrees.

Ryann tossed her large purse into the front passenger seat and focused her smile on him. "We're not late, are we?"

"Right on time." His focus slid to China.

A spark of surprised recognition showed in her eyes, but she just nodded and slipped into the backseat.

The tightness in his shoulders eased. The girl wore a ball cap, a sleeveless T-shirt, and a pair of tight jeans. Nothing out of the ordinary.

He pulled his Jeep Wrangler onto the main highway and headed out.

Ryann settled her shoulders against the seat. "Eric wanted to come."

"Did he?" Jake threw a glance her way. "Why?

This is not usually his type of gig."

"Yeah. I told him the other day we were going to check out the campground, and he said nothing." She glanced over her shoulder at China. "But when I mentioned yesterday that China was going—"

"Hey." China leaned into their space up front. "That kid is too narcissistic for me. Besides, how old is he? Eighteen? Nineteen? Too young."

"I think he's nineteen, but he likes you." Ryann's voice carried an undertone of laughter.

Jake looked in the rearview mirror in time to see China grimace.

She caught his gaze. "Look, where is this campground we're going to?"

"Juniper Springs. It's a federal recreation area in the Ocala National Forest. It's in the middle of the state, but north of Orlando, about a two-and-a-half-hour drive."

"What? Two and a half hours? You're kidding!" She yawned. "Maybe I'll take a nap then."

"It's too soon for that."

"Who says? I don't do early as a rule. Ryann showed up at my place, or I'd have never made it."

Ryann turned her head. "Well, Eric doesn't do early either, or he would have found a way to come."

"Would you leave the guy out of this?"

Jake watched China's eye roll and laughed. "I thought girls loved having guys fall all over them."

"You thought wrong. Let's talk about this campground and what we can expect—like, hopefully, hot water, showers, clean bathrooms…"

The girl had more questions than the teens' parents. One query had him thinking she knew camping, while the next made him think she was a novice. And the whole time he wondered if she just wanted to keep the conversation going for some reason he couldn't fathom. For sure, she never took the nap she'd mentioned.

༃

China pulled on her cap again. She'd worn it for
the Jeep ride, for the wind. All she needed was for it to go
sailing off, lost down this country road. No way could she
take a nap when she had to worry about the cap and her
hair.

Both sides of the road were lined with pines, in
neat rows, obviously planted—by the local Forest Service
or some lumber company. The earth smells and the wind
whipping through the open Jeep wooed her toward sleep,
so she sat forward and peppered Jake with more
questions.

At least he had answers. He'd obviously spent a
lot of time at this campground. Something they had in
common then—a love for the outdoors. Not that she'd
had it until six months ago.

She stared at the passing trees. They brought back
the last half-dozen months she'd spent camping in state
and national forests all over the southeast. When
Tanner's ultimatum drove her from her apartment, she
remembered a week she'd spent camping with a friend's
family after her dad had left, never to return, and the
peace that time had brought. So, with no place to live and
not much money, she'd bought a tent and headed out.
Luckily, the car was her own, even if the apartment
hadn't been.

She sighed. If she could stay awake and keep her
mind off the past, she'd get through the day just fine. She
fought the lump in her throat and thought of another
question for Jake.

When they arrived, Jake paid the entry fee, and
they headed down a wooden path lined by oaks, pines,
and palmettos. China followed behind Jake and Ryann.
Birds hopped from tree to tree. Their songs and the
squirrels rustling leaves in the bushes welcomed them.
She smiled and felt the tension drain to her feet and out.

The walkway wound past a bathhouse and spread out into a wide deck. Sloping ground beyond dropped to a large natural spring. Someone had used natural stones to form a barrier around the spring and had created a large swimming area. Most likely, the Forest Service again. Old oaks, their limbs heavy with Spanish moss, and palm trees shaded picnic tables around the pool.

They were early. No one had broken the pristine clarity of the water's surface yet.

Jake stopped abruptly, and she almost stumbled into him.

"Oh...my...goodness." Ryann's voice jumped two octaves. She threw her hands out, indicating the pool. "The water is gorgeous. Look at the colors, and it's so clear!"

Jake grinned. "I love this place."

"I can see why. Can we swim?"

He laughed. "Let's check the campground first. They have a few different areas. We'll see what you girls like, but I thought the one near another spring would fit us. It's near the oldest shelter, built, I think, back in the forties—if they haven't torn it down. There's higher ground there, in case it rains."

They walked to the edge of the pool.

"Yeah, you need that. Nothing like getting washed away in the middle of the night," China said.

Jake's head turned. "So, you have camped before."

"Is that shock I hear in your voice, Mr. Youth Pastor?"

He looked her up and down. "Not shock. Surprise, I guess."

"I bet I do a number of things that would surprise you."

"I bet you do."

She put her shoulders back. "You got a problem with me?"

"No. Why?"

She remembered how he'd turned and disappeared from church that first day. He was lying, but she didn't know what the problem was. Unless he'd listened to the gossip that she knew was circling the church like hyenas around a wounded gazelle.

"Well, you act like it." The man had looked her over this morning as if she were a wild animal that might bite.

She moved off and told herself not to be touchy. Across the pool, a wooden house stood, and next to it a large paddle wheel—as tall as the house. Water rushed over it, forcing it to move and turn. She watched the silver streams slap the boards. The sun flashed off the wet spray.

"Wow." Ryann threw her hand out again. "What did they use that for?"

"I've heard it was for electricity, but others say it's a mill wheel, used to turn equipment to grind grain. We'll be back. Let's head to the campground."

They walked past the large, spring-fed pool. The clear water would be enticing to most, but not to her. Besides, from what he said, the blue-green oasis was a shivering seventy-two degrees.

Jake led the way around the old mill and down a path that soon narrowed and forced them to walk single file. Palmettos, wild vines, and trees grew on both sides. The sound of the running water followed them.

When the root-strewn trail widened, she and Ryann walked two abreast. Jake brought up the rear. Birdsongs furnished a background for his running commentary on the park. He'd been camping here off and on since he was a kid.

China leaned close to Ryann. "I wonder how much farther it is. I think he should have warned us if we were going on an extensive hike."

"Heard that." Jake's voice sounded so close that

she jumped. "Don't tell me you're wimping out already."

"Never thought of wimping out, Mr. Youth Director."

"Good." Mock severity entered his voice. "If you're going to help with the youth, you'll need some stamina. Tell her, Ryann."

Ryann laughed. "You mean, like the time we went on a real hike not far from here and got lost?"

"Uh...well, that was a mix-up...in maps."

"A what?" China threw the question over her shoulder. "You took the wrong map?"

"I was *given* the wrong map."

Ryann tittered. "He freaked out when he realized we'd walked five miles out of our way, and it was getting dark."

"The idea of me freaking out—"

"It was our first excursion after he took over the youth, and we had three parents giving him the third degree when we didn't get to the campsite in time."

"We managed." Jake's defense jumped. "The jog back was good for all of us."

"I think some of us wondered if a heart attack was on the menu."

"You jogged all the way back? Five miles?" China let her voice rise in surprise.

"Not a full five, and we had breaks, and no one had a heart—"

Ryann cut him off. "Jogged through the swamp and the palmettos with full backpacks."

"Sounds more like Navy SEAL training than youth camp." China glanced over her shoulder again and grinned at Jake's expression.

Ryann's laughter echoed down the path, and other voices floated back to them. Three teenage girls appeared, heading their way. Golden skin was highlighted by brief bikinis. Three pairs of eyes skipped past China and Ryann and landed on Jake. Wide smiles materialized. She and Ryann stepped aside, and the girls sauntered past.

"Hi there," one of the girls said. Her gaze slid over Jake.

China chuckled, then lurched to the side as another person pushed past them.

"Well, excuse me." She stared after the man. He wore a ball cap and pulled it down as if nodding to her. Cheez!

She stumbled over a root and focused on the path again. A cool breeze touched the trees overhead, and the dappled shade shook and wavered. She savored the coolness. A bikini would have felt good today, but Ryann had clued her in that Jake was big on modesty for the youth group. Next time, though, she'd at least wear her shorts.

The path gave way to a large clearing. Two cement picnic tables sat to her right. On the left, crystal spring water glimmered at them. A wooden bridge arched over the water's center. Heavy oak limbs stretched above it.

"Oh, I like it." China picked up her pace and headed for the bridge.

"The shelter on the other side is broken down, I think. But we can camp around the bend, right past it."

As she stepped onto the bridge, a movement on the water's edge startled her. She stopped and stared. Someone lay on the ground. As she stared, the person began to slide backward toward the water. She blinked. A dark, heavy tail came into view, ridges running down its edge. She gasped and lifted her hand to her mouth.

Ryann and Jake stepped up next to her.

"What's up?" Jake asked. "Oh, an alligator."

China grabbed his arm. "He's got someone in his mouth."

"What?"

"Look! Look at him!"

The alligator slipped beneath the surface, pulling the person with him. The wash of the water lapping the shore reached them.

Ryann shrieked.

Jake spun their way. "China, call 911. Ryann, run back to the bathhouse near the entrance and get help."

He kicked off his sandals, sprinted from the bridge, and skidded to a stop right where the alligator vanished. A moment later, he made a shallow dive into the spring and disappeared.

China sucked in her breath. She yanked her phone from her jeans pocket and pushed 911.

Chapter 2

China shoved the phone back into her jeans pocket. The call had actually gone through. Help was on the way but would take too long to arrive. They'd driven thirty miles from Ocala out into the forest. Heart pounding like a sledge hammer, she leaned as far over the railing as she could and prayed.

Jake surfaced a moment later. He gulped air and dove again. China saw the alligator ahead of him—a smeared but recognizable shape through the clear water. On either side of its massive head, the body of a man protruded. The creature headed away from the bridge. China cringed and choked back a scream.

Jake broke the surface again and swam furiously on top of the water, the slap and spray echoing across the clearing. He was right above the reptile when he dove a third time.

"Oh God, please help. Oh God, oh God." China's words tumbled over themselves, her prayer a desperate plea.

Beneath the surface, the figures melded together, and the waters clouded. Sand and eelgrass swirled.

Words came now. "Lord, keep him safe. Help him, please."

Jake's legs appeared, thrashing, water flying, then disappeared. The gator's tail flew up and slapped down. A scream rose in China's throat. An arm surfaced, then Jake's head. He gasped for air and vanished once more. Another heartbeat passed. All was quiet.

China's grip strangled the railing. "Jake!"

The surface burst, and Jake's hair and broad

shoulders shot upward. He heaved sideways and yanked another head and shoulders into the air. The head lolled back and down. Treading water, Jake moved and shifted until he had his arm across the man's chest, his other hand gripping the victim's arm.

China's heart leapt. She raced from the far side of the bridge to the edge of the spring. Jake sidestroked, swimming her way. China eyed the water in back and beneath him. Would the alligator return? Her heart hammered. Jake stood chest deep in the water, shifted his grip, and began to drag the person ashore.

China stepped tentatively into the water and grabbed the man's hand. The heavy, lifeless feel of it jerked a cry from her throat, and she dropped it.

Jake lifted his head, water sliding in rivulets down his face. "We'll try CPR, but I think...I think he's dead."

❦

Dead.

China put her head in her hands. She sat on the hard bench away from the body, the Sheriff's officers, and the newswoman.

She'd emptied her stomach in the bushes right after she and Jake pulled the body ashore. The man's eyes stared at her from his swollen face, like something out of the *Walking Dead*. She shuddered and huddled in on herself, feeling cold even in the mid-eighties temperature.

Jake had risked his life for someone already dead—and not from drowning or from the alligator, but, from what they could see, a bullet to his chest. The group from the Sheriff's Office would confirm that—one way or the other.

Movement close by wrenched her head up. Jake and the detective approached. Ryann sat on another bench across from her. She gave China an encouraging

smile. Near the water, a deputy and a couple other people
searched the brush and put out little yellow stands for
evidence markers.

Forensics. Yeah.

"China, this is Detective Burke. He's got some
questions for you."

She tried a nod, but it didn't quite succeed.

Jake sat next to her. "You okay?"

She gave a short shake of her head but
straightened and eyed the detective.

"Miss Summers, I understand you were with Mr.
Osborne and Miss Byrd on the path between the pool area
and here when three young ladies passed you."

She sent a look Jake's way. "The girls?"

"Yes. Mr. Osborne said three young ladies passed
you. We sent a man to the pool area to see if he could
find them, but he hasn't yet. Could you describe them?"

China gave a brief description. The detective
wrote in a small book. "That matches the others'
descriptions. Did you see anyone else?"

"Sure. The man following them."

"A man was following them?"

"Well, he was coming behind them."

"Coming behind or following? Mr. Osborne felt
the man might actually be following the young ladies. Is
that what you meant?"

"No, I…" She glanced at Jake. "You know, Jake's
a youth pastor. Any man hanging around young girls is
probably suspicious to him."

Jake frowned, and China smiled. "You have to
admit that, Jake. Ryann said you were on the
conservative side."

He made a noise of disagreement.

"But you didn't think anything sinister about it?"
the detective asked China.

"Not really. He seemed in a hurry though, and he
knocked into me."

"Can you describe him? His clothes, anything else you remember."

China blinked. "A hat." When the detective said nothing, she shrugged. "I mean, he had some clothes on, of course. Shorts, I think. I remember the ball cap because I had on one, too. Oh, and he had scraggly gray hair—like down to his shoulders. Dirty looking."

"What color was the ball cap? Any wording?"

China thought back. "Red, I think. And maybe some wording, but I don't remember what it was. I'm sorry. I'm not very good at this."

"Did you get a look at his face?"

"No, he pulled the ball cap low and kind of turned his head away. I do remember that."

"That was Mr. Osborne's feeling, too. Okay. Is there anything else you can remember? Anything you heard or saw when you got here or while you were on the bridge?"

"Nothing." She glanced sideways. "I just worried about Jake."

"Sam." A voice penetrated their threesome. "We've got something here. Want to take a look?"

The detective looked around. "Okay. Coming." He pocketed his book, nodded to them, and strolled in the direction of the water.

"You're cold, aren't you?" Jake asked China.

"Yeah. How could you tell? The chattering of my teeth?"

A smile pulled the corner of his mouth. "That would about do it."

Ryann rose and stepped in front of them. "You think they're through with us? You think we could go?"

"I'll ask." Jake stood.

A woman in a tight blue dress and heels approached. "Mr. Osborne, I'm Lil Duram with WJPY News. I'd like to talk with you." She held up a small microphone and a camera. "Why would you risk your life for someone you didn't know?"

"I don't have an answer for that. You just do it."

"You just do it? Jump in the water with an alligator?"

"Jake's with the Coast Guard," Ryann said. "It's what he does—saving people."

"The Coast Guard?" Lil held the microphone closer. "We're doing a big media event in a couple of weeks on first responders, and that includes the Coast Guard. So, are you a rescue swimmer?"

Jake threw a scowl Ryann's way. "No, I'm a pilot."

"Wow. Tell me…"

"Look, we're ready to leave. Can't you get whatever information you need from the Sheriff's deputy or the detective?"

"What I want is a personal story. You're a hero, and those watching on the news tonight will want to know more about you."

"I'm sorry. I'm not a hero. I'm just a person who happened by at the right time."

"But you save lives in the Coast Guard? How was this different?" She waved the mic again.

"It was different because I didn't save anybody. The man was dead before I got to him."

"It sounds like this was hard for you. Have you done that before with the Coast Guard? Found someone that—"

Jake cut her off. "We deal with both life and death situations daily. Now—"

"But I'm sure you've never—"

"Look, Lil." China came off the bench and stepped up next to Jake. "You've got a lot of questions, but we're ready to leave. It's been tough here. Why don't you just get your information from the police?"

The mic swung her way. "And you're…" The woman's eyes went to a small tablet she held in her other hand. "China Summers, right? You helped Mr. Osborne pull the body ashore? Did you see anything—"

"I'm sorry, but I'm not talking about it—with anyone but the police." She turned to Jake. "Can you see if we can leave?"

"Yeah."

China caught the thank-you in his eyes before he walked away. She grabbed Ryann's arm. "Let's go stand over there." She pointed to some shade under one of the oaks.

"Well, you'll be on the news tonight," the reporter called after them. "I'm sure this story won't get buried."

৵

The bedside clock read 10:00 PM. Jake clasped his wrist in his other hand and stretched it over his head. The bed and the cool sheets made an oasis of comfort beneath him. Something he needed. He'd talked with Zeke, given him a quick briefing before anyone saw the news, and asked him to spread it to the others. Hopefully, that would stop a flood of phone calls from friends wanting to know more. And Zeke understood the frustration Jake had felt pulling someone dead from the waters.

The reporter had touched a nerve asking about it. Not one of them wanted to arrive too late to help someone. He sighed. Being late meant someone died, someone who had family and loved ones.

He wasn't a hero.

Besides, alligators were opportunists—as he'd told China and Ryann on the way home. He was glad he'd brought the man's body to the surface, glad an ID could be made rather than letting the man disappear forever down Juniper Run or down the throat of the gator. Whoever he was, the man had lived and loved and probably was loved by someone. How he wound up shot in the middle of the Ocala National Forest was for the police to figure out.

But would any sane person murder someone where anyone might see them? He'd heard the detective and one of the forensic crew talk about the time of death. Rigor mortis had not set in, so, they'd guessed the time at around an hour or two before Jake and the others arrived. Although the water temperature could throw that off.

Jake scrunched his pillow. If they'd arrived at the springs sooner, would they have ended the same way? That thought ramped his heartbeat. He and Ryann and China—and perhaps the other three girls. The police had tried to track them down, but to no avail. And the man had disappeared, too. A man who had pulled his hat down as he passed them...

He glanced at the clock again. He'd been up since 5:00 AM. A long day even if you didn't count the huge stress of pulling a man from a gator's mouth. He needed some rest before his shift tomorrow.

The phone rang. He picked it up from the bedside table, glanced at the face, and groaned. Sleep wasn't going to happen.

"Yeah?"

"They're calling us in, Jake." Zeke's voice sounded charged. "A man radioed in a mayday earlier. He had a twenty-nine-foot sailboat taking on water, and four family members with him. His wife and three kids. The boat sunk. The first crew rescued three survivors. They haven't found the other two, and the wind's getting up. We're the second unit."

"All right. I'm on the way." He dropped the phone and pushed up from the bed. Zeke didn't have to say more. The wind rising meant the swells and the whitecaps would increase. Both added obstacles to the search.

A few minutes later, dressed and with a tall coffee in his hand, Jake flipped on the outside light and headed for the front door. He leapt the steps. From somewhere, a muffled *phst* sounded. A bee went by his ear. Something chipped the cement construction block behind him. He jerked to a stop. Another *phst* sounded, and something embedded itself into his Jeep.

Someone was shooting at him. With a silencer.

He dove behind the front bumper. No, that was crazy. He turned his head, listened. No car had passed. Not a random drive-by then. He had to be mistaken. He set the coffee to the side, slumped lower, and looked under the Jeep to the road and the yard opposite his.

Across the street, a dog barked. Jake flattened himself against the driveway and inched forward under the Jeep. The dog's barking increased. A man's voice, from inside the house, yelled, "Shut up!" and then, in the light from the streetlamp, Jake saw movement near the house. A figure darted from the side yard and raced down the road, away from him.

Jake hauled himself out from under the Jeep and jumped to his feet. Adrenaline surged, but he forced himself to stand still. It wouldn't do any good—unless he wanted to get killed. The man had a gun, and Jake had nothing. He ground his teeth, then swung around and tried to see the indentation in the block wall.

If he hadn't jumped the steps, he might be dead.

The next instant, he dug his phone from his pocket and hit 911.

꙳

The chopper lifted off the pad into the night. They were an hour late getting up. The police had had a lot of questions. Twice in the same day he'd been involved in some type of shooting. Even *he* had questions, but getting to the station had weighed on him, and he'd pressed the officers to get away.

The first crew was headed back low on gas. The third crew's pilot was out of town. Jake ground his teeth. They needed to find these two people while there was a chance of finding them alive.

Earlier, after the mayday, a small rescue boat and a helo had deployed. The dad was instructed to keep everyone in the area around the boat and to ignite the flare as the rescue team approached. Coast Guard crew members had followed the flash of a red flare to the sinking sailboat, about ten miles west of Clearwater Beach, around 7:00 PM.

All five in the family—dad, mother, two teen boys, one ten-year-old girl—had life jackets. The father, daughter, and one son were rescued, but the man's wife and the other son were separated from the rest. The father said his older son injured his arm when they jumped from the boat. He'd slipped and cracked his elbow against the side of the boat as he'd fallen into the water. His wife held on to him while the dad held the other two children. After a while though the seas picked up, and the two groups drifted apart.

Officials had established a grid pattern, which Jake and his crew had crisscrossed eight times now. The April Gulf temperatures were in the low seventies. Not a good situation for those in the water. They always worried about hypothermia, and in these conditions, it could set in within three or four hours—and it could kill. Jake rolled his shoulders, the heaviness from the search and his tiredness pressing on them m like forty-pound dumbbells.

Charley Ford glanced his way. "You okay?"

"Yeah. A long day, and this is anything but a picnic tonight." The mother and the teen were out here somewhere. They just needed to find them.

Charley gave a brief nod. "I heard about your alligator rescue."

"Not a rescue."

"Well, man, from what I heard—"

"Not a rescue." Jake kept his eyes forward.

"Listen, you can't help it if the man was—"

"Mark, mark, mark." The flight mechanic's voice interrupted. "Ten o'clock. Ten o'clock. One person in the water."

Jake brought the helo around.

"One?" Charley's voice mimicked Jake's thinking.

"Forward and right 40."

Jake adjusted the stick. The huge spotlight cut into the night. Below them, the dark sea whipped; the whitecaps rose and tossed.

"We'll harness Zeke," the flight mechanic said. "Survivor looks...unconscious."

That didn't sound good. Hypothermia in the Gulf waters was real, no matter what time of year. Even with a life vest, hypothermia could kill. Charley unhooked his own harness and stepped to the back.

"Rescue checklist complete. Swimmer going down."

Quiet followed except for the whump-whump of the blades.

"Swimmer's away. Swimmer's okay."

The night seemed to darken as they waited.

"Swimmer's calling for the litter."

Jake tightened his grip on the stick. No indication from Zeke then about the person's condition.

"Trail line is connected. Litter out the door."

"Forward and right 10."

The silence stretched, then, "Litter's on the way up." A pause. "Litter's below cabin door." A long pause. "Hoist complete."

Charley's voice mixed with the flight mechanic's—the quick question and answer themselves telling. More movement and shuffling. Charley and the flight mechanic were working on him or her, Jake knew, but were they just following procedure, or was the person alive?

A few minutes later, the mechanic's voice came

again. "Bringing up rescue swimmer.

"Hold position. Hold. Swimmer's below cabin door."

The movement and shift as Zeke came on board filled his ears. *Come on, guys...*

"Cabin door closed. Ready for forward flight."

Charley made his way forward and, slipped into his seat. He glanced Jake's way and shook his head.

A hard mass dropped into Jake's stomach. They hadn't gotten here in time. Two in twenty-four hours. He'd lost two.

Chapter 3

Morning sun poured through the passenger side window of the Jeep. Jake hit the steering wheel. This family had had their safety measures and the equipment they needed, and they'd still lost one—possibly two—members. How had they not found her in time? Because he was late? Because someone had shot at him? *Why?* He asked God the same question almost every time. Would he ever get an answer?

The chances of the teen being alive were slim, but the mother had been model thin, and she'd been in the water close to five hours when they'd found her. The teen, the dad said, was muscular and close to six feet. Hypothermia would take longer. Hopefully, the third team would find him. If they did, would the boy ever forget? Would he blame himself for his mother's death?

Jake pulled into his driveway. He started to step from the Jeep, then stopped. Caution fingered up his spine. He backed the Jeep out of the drive and glanced up and down the street and into his neighbors' yards as well as his own. At last, he turned the Jeep and backed into his driveway.

He threw open the door to his Jeep and cautiously walked to the front of his house. Once inside he took a deep breath. Exhaustion rode in his arms and legs and stretched to every part of his body.

He stood in his living area, emptiness spreading through him as it used to do years ago. What next? The forty-pound weights on his shoulders seemed to have doubled. Sleep would be welcome, but would it come?

He walked to the kitchen. No. No food. He

turned, went to his office, and stood again. He should call someone. Zeke or Charley. Alan, maybe.

He shoved his hands into his pockets. Wasn't he, Jake, supposed to be the spiritual one in the crew? Hadn't he always presented himself as the one with the answers? The weight in his chest returned.

I don't have answers, Lord. I want them myself.

He leaned over and pushed the button on his computer. The blue screen popped on, glowing in the dark. At least this worked.

When he sat, he put his head in his hands. After a short time, his hand clicked through what was needed to bring up the internet. He hesitated. What he wanted was to get his mind off the whole situation…

He swallowed. His hands froze over the keyboard. What was he doing? His breathing came in fits and starts. He could lose himself in it. Forget that they hadn't found the woman in time or the man in the alligator's mouth. The crazy newsperson had called him a hero. A hero! All he'd done was rescue a body, and that was all they'd done today.

China's face rose in his memory. She'd gone and thrown up as soon as they'd pulled the man's body ashore.

China.

The tattoo.

The porn star…

He focused on the computer screen, and his hands played over the keyboard. He needed a release, something to get him past the depression. He hadn't signed on for this, hadn't let himself think that it would be part of the job. And every time it happened, the memories returned.

Jake stared at the screen. He bowed his head and tried to shove the thoughts back that rose every time they pulled someone dead from the waters.

They'd never found his dad. Why couldn't he

forget? Or forgive himself? Logically, at ten he couldn't be held responsible for his father's death. But Jake had insisted on going fishing that day. It was his birthday, after all. Even though a storm was coming, even though his dad had said no the first time, when his dad finally gave in, Jake had been so ecstatic. And then the storm rose…

When a friend showed him a few sexy sites at age eleven, he'd found more than a solution for his rising hormones—he'd found something that helped him forget his guilt, something that quickly became an addiction, until three years ago.

Get up. Get out.

The tight grip of hardened muscles across his shoulders sent pain through his neck and head. He narrowed his eyes against the pain and rolled his head side to side, then glanced again at the computer screen.

This would not help. *This won't bring your dad back. Won't bring the woman back. It just adds to your problems.*

Jake jerked back from the keyboard and thrust himself away from the desk. His hands shot out and across the desk. The laptop toppled and crashed to the floor. A coffee cup he'd sat there two days earlier spewed dark liquid onto the wooden floor. Papers and pens and sticky notes scattered.

"No! Do you hear me? No!"

He grabbed his keys and phone and sprinted to the front door. Before he thought about looking around, he'd climbed into the front seat of the Jeep and started for the street. His peripheral vision caught a shape to his right, and Jake slammed on his the brakes. A kid riding a bike stopped and stared at him.

Jake gritted his teeth. *It's a neighborhood, J.T. Slow down.* He put the Jeep in drive and passed the kid slowly. His hand closed on the phone, and he hit speed dial.

"Hello?" Pastor Alan's voice sounded winded and a little short. "Jake?"

"Yeah."

"I'm right in the middle of helping John with a tree that came down. Can it wait?"

Jake squinted at the road and tightened his grip on the wheel. "No."

"No?" He heard the other man take a hard breath. "John, take this, will you? And take a break." Other noises, then the pastor's voice again. "Okay, Jake. I'm free. What's up?"

Jake swallowed. "I'm having some trouble here. Life is a… Well, let's just say that the last twenty-four hours have been deadly."

"Deadly? Are we talking real life? You lose someone, or temptation is staring you in the face?"

"Both."

"Both?" The man's voice changed. "Okay… Come to John's place."

"No, listen. I'm not sure…"

"No, you listen to me. I don't know about the person you lost, but I know in another area you're fighting a war that's already been won. You are redeemed. Get over here and live like it. No one's condemning you but the enemy."

Jake said nothing.

Pastor Alan cleared his throat. "And tell us about the person you lost. We'll be waiting."

❧

Both Pastor Alan and John turned as Jake walked up. Jake nodded. He didn't know if Alan had shared anything with John, but if another person had to know his past, John would be one of the better ones.

John set down the chain saw on a nearby bench and straightened. The man was a few inches taller than Jake, well built, a little thin, but it was the eyes and voice that drew people. Eyes and a voice that said he cared.

Jake nodded again and smiled. The tension had begun to erode as he drove here. Now it fell from his shoulders.

"Hope you don't mind if I drop in."

"Only if you mind being put to work," John said.

Jake eyed the tree then let his focus veer to the pastor. "I was never afraid of hard work."

Pastor Alan grinned. "Good thing, because that's usually what John has for me when he calls for help."

John slapped the pastor on the back. "I have to get you out of that office once in a while." His glance rested on Jake again. "We heard that the Coast Guard pulled a body from the Gulf today. One of the family from that sailboat?"

"Yeah." Jake caught his voice, steadied it. "The wife, mother." He shook his head. "I hate pulling bodies from the water. I got in this to save lives."

John grunted. "I understand that."

"Yeah, I suppose you do. Working against human trafficking saves women from a new type of slavery."

Alan leaned against the tree's trunk. "You know, I haven't said anything to John, but if you don't mind, he might make a good anchor for this group."

"I'd thought about that. I'm fine with it. Although calling it a group is maybe a stretch."

Alan crossed his arms. "I'm thinking group. I'm thinking that more than you—and I—have had this problem. In fact, I know it. The percentages are the same everywhere—fifty to eighty percent of men struggle with pornography, even in the church." He glanced at John. "Only a few don't."

Jake's look rested on John. "You don't?"

"Pornography? No. One of the few, I guess. I don't know how I can be of help, but you know about Alan's struggle?" His gaze ricocheted from Jake to Alan. Alan nodded. "Right after he came to Christ twenty years ago—when no one talked about it—Daneen found out. Praise God she didn't leave him or act like it was normal either. She helped him walk out of it. With God's help, he's been clean—as far as I know—for twenty years."

"Almost twenty years," Alan said. "John's my accountability partner. He can help just by being here reminding us that not everyone has to have this struggle. That we can teach our children while they're young how dangerous it is. And it is dangerous. To marriages, to relationships, to those caught in it. Just like every other addiction."

Jake cleared his throat. "So, what are you suggesting?"

"It would entail you 'coming out,' as it were. Talking about your struggle with porn. Telling the church how you got free. Letting them know we're starting a support and mentor group for others."

"I was up front with you when you hired me— about my past struggles with internet pornography and where I was, and you understood. But telling the whole church is something different."

"A lot of youth pastors and lead pastors struggle with the same thing but are never up front with it. You told me the truth. That's why I hired you. That and the fact you'd been clean for three years, and I would be your accountability partner."

Jake nodded. "Until today."

Alan straightened. "Today?"

"The temptation was right there—after I got back from the station, after losing the mom, someone shooting at me, the alligator incident." And China. But he didn't say that.

"You've slipped back then?" John's voice, measured but calm.

Jake shook his head. "No. I crashed the laptop instead and came here." He gave a forced grin. "Literally. Tossed it on the floor."

John's grin wasn't forced. "Good for you."

"Yeah, but now I'll have to replace it."

"You're sure you want to?"

Jake laughed. "That's a question I need to consider."

"And you and Alan both need to consider what the church will think if you 'go public' with this." John shot a glance from Jake to Alan. "You'll lose members—both in the youth and in the general congregation."

Alan nodded. "I've thought about this for a while, and you're right. But the other choice is to leave things as they are, never mention it, hide it, and give no help. I can't do that anymore. The Church has always run from hard situations—and this *is* hard. But God never meant us to do that. We need to face it and meet it head on. Pornography is not only a sin—it's a scourge. It allows women and children to be abused for a man's entertainment or psychological need. It often leads to real abuse and is a cause of sex trafficking. It also enslaves the men—and women—addicted to it."

Jake swallowed. He knew this and found it repulsive. How could the temptation still rise to taunt him?

Alan put a hand on his arm. "We're all in a battle of some kind as long as we're on this earth. But remember who you are—a soldier, a warrior for Christ. He never leaves you. He battles with you. Because of Him, you conquered this, and you hold to that win with Him. He has not stopped loving you and never will."

"Thank you. I need that reminder."

"It'll keep you humble."

"It will." He looked around and studied the fallen tree. "Well, what can I do to get this project back on the road?"

"I'm sure John has an idea, but wait a moment. Let's back up here, son. What do you mean about someone shooting at you?"

≀♦

China didn't expect the knock on her door. She certainly didn't expect the person now standing on her threshold.

Her voice dropped almost to a whisper. "Hello, Sharee."

Sharee smiled at her—tentative, a little crooked. "Hi, China." A moment of silence held between them. "Can I come in?"

"Uh, sure." China waved past her, indicating the living area. "Yeah, come in. Have a seat." She opened the door farther, backing away.

Sharee glanced around. "Wow. I like your pictures. Have you been to all these places?"

China closed the door. "Yes. State parks in most of the southeast states. I…I camped a lot over the last six months. Surprised?"

Sharee slid onto one of a pair of barrel chairs, slid her purse on the floor, and curled up. "Yes, I guess I am."

"Well, I was, too. At least I didn't think I'd like it, but I did. So, I just decided to visit as many as possible—explore, you know." She stood near the door still and shifted from one foot to another. What was Sharee doing here? Should she offer her something to drink, to eat?

"Lonely, though…unless…you were with someone." Sharee waved to the other chair. "Why don't you sit down?"

China nodded. Invited to sit down in her own home… She dropped onto the other barrel chair. "Okay."

"So, you spent six months camping throughout the southeast and then came back home?"

"Yes."

Sharee nodded but said nothing more.

China cleared her throat. "Actually, it was because of the camping—alone. The quiet and time for reflection that—in the end—drew me back here." She wasn't going to tell this woman about Tanner and the healing God had done in her life. But Sharee looked like she was going to stay for a while. Why had she come?

"I guess you're wondering why I'm here."

"Yeah. Just thinking that."

"The last time I saw you, you had a lot to say. I'm sure you remember."

Oh yeah. She remembered. Like she remembered the other things, the other people she'd hurt in the church. Is this why God had brought her back? To make amends to all these people? She swallowed again. It had always been hard for her to say "I'm sorry." Was that what God required of her?

"I need to know where you are in life now." Sharee's voice wavered, but she straightened in the chair. "China, I don't want to cause you problems, but I don't want you to cause me any either. John and I are married. We have a baby. You know that. I need to know if I have anything to worry about from you."

Well, there it was. Out there. Right away. Should she apologize?

"I've forgiven you—and so has John—for your actions before."

Well, they'd forgiven her. No need to humble herself then, to "eat crow," as they say. "John knows you're here?"

"Yes. He and I are very open in our communication. I know you tried to seduce him before he and I married, and you told me later that it was a game."

Yep. The woman's words hit the bull's-eye, even though it seemed a long time ago. The person she'd been back then, well… She cleared her throat. "I guess I should apologize."

Sharee said nothing.

Great. Okay. "I do. I apologize. I know what I did was wrong, and it wasn't just to you and John."

"You might want to apologize to those you really

hurt. You caused some problems for John and me, but you didn't hurt us."

China nodded. The thought of apologizing to everyone sent a cold, knifelike pain into her gut.

Sharee leaned forward in the chair. "John thought you might have changed. That's why he agreed that I should come talk with you."

Great. China dropped her head and shifted in her chair again. Just what she wanted. A psychoanalysis.

"Have you changed?"

"What?" She pulled her head up, startled. The voice and question seemed to echo deep in her soul.

Sharee repeated her question. "Have you changed?"

"Of course I have." She was no longer answering Sharee, but that voice inside her. "I've given my life to you…I mean, I've given my life to God. He brought me back here."

Sharee's mouth arched upward. "I am so glad to hear that. John will be glad, too. He's been praying for you ever since we married. It was a little harder for me at first, but I have, too."

China wasn't sure what to say to that. Okay. They'd married, gone overseas as missionaries, had a baby—and still thought about her?

"I…thank you." She put her hands in her lap. "Where is the baby, by the way?"

"With Ryann. You know how she loves babies."

"Yeah. So sad about her miscarriage. I…it was just one of the things at the time that made me wonder if there was a God. You know, the same question everyone has. If God is real and so powerful and so loving, why do these things happen?"

Sharee clasped her hands in her lap, too. "Yeah, we all wonder that, don't we? Of course, this is not a perfect place. God has allowed evil in the world, then He gives us a choice—to choose one or the other. And He's put sowing and reaping in the earth. We reap from our good or bad choices. But we don't like reaping from our bad choices, do we? We give in to the wrong thing—to our ungodly desires—and then expect God to miraculously get us out of whatever mess we find ourselves in."

China gave a weak grin. "Yes. I think that's what I expected Him to do."

"Still, there's a lot we don't understand. Faith in God includes trusting Him even when we don't understand. But look—did you hear about the miracle surrounding little Johnnie's birth?"

"No, I…"

Knock. Knock. Knock.

China glanced at the door. "Now who could that be? I hardly ever have anyone come here. Two in one day is a surprise." She rose and went to the door.

"Ms. Summers?"

The man standing there was no one she knew, but she saw the news van behind him and the microphone in his hand. "Look, I told the other lady that I was not talking with anyone."

"I just have a few questions about your part in the alligator story. I…"

"I said I wasn't talking with anyone." She shoved at the door, but the man leaned in and thrust it back.

"I just have a few questions."

"I said no."

"If you'll let me come in…"

"No, and let go of the door!"

"Look, sweetheart, I—"

"She said no." Sharee's voice came from behind her. "And if you try to force your way in here, I'll call the police."

The man jerked his head up, hesitated, then stepped backward. He eyed China. "I thought you lived alone."

"Get out of here." China thrust against his chest until he took another step back. She pushed the door closed. "Wow. What a jerk." She scrambled to the front window in time to see him climb into a black Dodge van and drive away. "He's got the same call letters on that van as the other lady."

"Maybe he was trying to scoop her story."

China glanced back at Sharee. "Maybe. I'm glad you were here though. That surprised him."

"Yes, it did."

"Where's your car?"

"Oh." Sharee came to the window and pointed down the street. "I parked on the other side and down one house—in the shade."

"You know what? I'm going to call that lady and tell her about this guy—and reiterate that I'm not going to be interviewed by anyone."

Sharee grinned. "Go for it."

A few minutes later, she set the phone down and stared at Sharee. "Did you hear that?"

Sharee's brows knitted. "I think so. They don't have a reporter like the one you described?"

"No, they don't. And they don't have Dodge vans either. All their vans are Fords."

Chapter 4

The kid was alive.

Jake fought to keep his emotions from soaring too high and to keep the helicopter's hover as Zeke prepared to go out the door. If Zeke's adrenaline rush was the same as Jake's and *if* they were over water, Zeke might jump out the door—no hoist needed. As it was, they had a ground landing to prepare for.

The teen had somehow made it to one of the many small islands sprinkled off the coastline. For two days he'd survived. How bad he was—dehydrated, sunburned, and with an injured arm—Jake didn't know. But alive nonetheless.

"Swimmer's down. Swimmer's landed."

Landed. Brush and birds covered the small island that was a rookery for a dozen species of birds. The ground where Zeke and the teen were standing must be inches deep in bird droppings. Earlier in the day, Jake had prayed about their flight pattern. God seemed to be leading him to expand it. The crew agreed to divert, and they'd found the boy within hours. Jake shook his head and smiled. God's hand.

"Swimmer's calling for the basket."

Charley had an ear-to-ear grin. "Can't wait to bring this one in."

"I'm with you. Bet he has a story to tell."

Charley unhooked his harness. "That's a sure thing. Wonder if he's been right here for three days."

"Zeke's finding out."

"Yep." Charley made his way to the back.

"Trail line is connected. Basket going out the

door." The flight mechanic's voice interrupted. "Right five. Stop and hold."

Quiet filled the cabin. Jake waited for the flight mechanic's litany to start again, but the silence stretched. He tried to envision what might be wrong. Was the boy's injury more serious than they'd been told? In the pilot's position, he couldn't see what happened below. The helo's blades created a wind that someone dehydrated and hurt would find hard to stand against, but Zeke would take care of that. Zeke hadn't graduated the Coast Guard's equivalent to the Navy SEAL's swimmers' school to let something like this defeat him.

"Survivor's in basket. Survivor's coming up."

Jake nodded his head and grinned. *Thank you, Lord!* What a word. *Survivor.*

"Basket below cabin door. Basket at the door. Survivor's in cabin."

Jake tightened his grip on the cyclic stick and kept the MH-60 Jayhawk hovering in place as he followed what was happening in back. The rustle as they lifted the teen from the basket, the question and answer, checking his vitals, getting an IV started...

Charley's voice reached Jake. "You're okay now. Your dad and siblings are fine."

The mechanics words cut across Charley's. "Easy right and hold. Bringing swimmer up." A minute later, "Swimmer below cabin door. Swimmer's in the cabin. Hoist complete."

Jake waited for the last of the checklist. In the back, the tone of the voices changed. Question and answer again. He cocked his head. Charley's words were unintelligible, but the kid's voice jumped, and he began to wail.

"Cabin door closed."

"Take her home, J.T."

Jake brought the Jayhawk around, his head still tilted to hear the commotion in the back.

Charley slipped into his seat and gave a slow shake of his head. "The kid asked about his family, asked about his mom."

Jake nodded. Of course he had. The euphoria of finding the boy dropped.

Charley radioed for an ambulance to meet them and for someone to inform the family.

The boy sobbed part of the way back. The quiet before they landed disturbed Jake. He could imagine the guilt. He'd felt the same way when he was rescued. They'd never found his dad.

Below them, an ambulance pulled into the station. In another few minutes, the helo landed and the paramedics approached with a gurney.

He watched in silence for a moment. "What's the boy's name again?"

"Mose."

Jake climbed from the chopper and went around to the gurney. The flight mechanic and Zeke worked with the paramedics to get the teen transferred. Jake had confidence in his team. They'd regulated the kid's temperature and started the IV, did what was needed. The boy would make it. Physically.

Jake leaned over him. "How you feeling, Mose?"

The teen opened his eyes, stared upward, then shut them. Jake leaned closer. "Your dad, sister, and brother will be waiting for you at the hospital."

The teen gave a brief nod but didn't look at him.

Jake moved out of the medic's way but stepped back immediately. "I lost my dad at ten."

Mose's eyes opened and caught Jake's for an instant.

"To the sea."

The teen's gaze slid back to Jake's. His eyes were round, filled with sadness that grabbed at Jake's throat. He clamped a hand on the boy's arm. The paramedic tried to push him out of the way, but Jake cut him a quick look, and the medic moved around him.

"I thought it was my fault, you see. It had to be my fault because I'd talked him into going out that day. But I've been doing this"—he waved at the helicopter—"a few years now. And some things just happen. No way to predict it. You can't blame yourself."

"I couldn't hold on." The teen's words came rough and uneven.

"Whether you could or not, you can't help hypothermia or the high seas that day. In your mom's case, hypothermia set it in. And when that happens, your body begins to shut down. You can lose consciousness, which is probably what happened to your mom. Holding on wouldn't have mattered."

Mose's throat worked. "I was stronger. I should have…"

"You injured your arm and were hypothermic, too, no doubt. Your muscles and extra body weight saved you."

Tears made their way from the corner of the boy's dark-brown eyes. He shoved the back of a hand against them.

The paramedic pushed against Jake one more time. "We've got to get him to the hospital."

Jake stepped back. "Your dad is ecstatic that you were found. I'm sorry about your mom." He took a deep breath. "I really am. But it wasn't your fault."

The teen closed his eyes and nodded as the paramedics pushed him toward the ambulance.

And this isn't a perfect world, he wanted to say. *Heaven awaits, but this isn't it.* Jake dropped his head. Guilt battled with the words he'd just told the boy. If he knew it was true for Mose, why couldn't he believe it for himself?

っ♥

The church was full. Unusual for a Sunday night,

but Jake wasn't surprised. Once Pastor Alan had made it known that there would be a discussion about the youth leadership, all parents and grandparents had come—some bringing their teens, some forcing them to stay at home.

Not only were his shoulders tight tonight, but someone must have taken a socket wrench and ratcheted up the muscles in his calves, thighs, and stomach too.

His eyes roved the congregation, digesting their expressions, before he continued. "Many men—many in the church—struggle with pornography. Some more than others. For me, Satan had me bound and delivered. I didn't see it as a problem. Most men don't. It took a girlfriend slamming me with my lack of relationship, challenging my Christianity, and telling me that I, and men like me, were what fueled the billion-dollar business of sex trafficking that really got me to look at myself."

"And how do we know that you're not into pornography anymore?"

Jake took a deep breath and slid his focus from the woman in red to Pastor Alan for a moment. John sat on the pastor's left, Daneen on his right. Alan nodded encouragement, as he'd done for the last hour. After Pastor Alan's announcement of a special Sunday night meeting, and after his explanation about the David's Mighty Men group, as he'd named it, he'd given his testimony, then asked Jake to give his.

The difference between a twenty-year recovery in Alan's case and a three-year recovery in his own had been pointed out numerous times already. The congregation had fine-tuned their grilling on Jake after questioning Alan for twenty minutes.

"Again, Alan, and now John, are my accountability partners. They both have access to my computer at any time. Alan has since I was hired. Lately, we installed Covenant Eyes on it so they can see every place I visit online."

"Well, John and Sharee are going back to

Indonesia in a few months. And you could have another computer or another phone that they don't know about."

"If I'd wanted to keep this hidden, I wouldn't have said anything to Alan in the first place."

"I don't like it. I don't like someone who has trouble with pornography having anything to do with my daughter." The woman in red crossed her arms over her chest.

Jake wanted to drop his head but didn't. Standing in front of them all, giving up the secrecy and privacy of his life, had torn him. Their once good opinion of him had shredded, and it would take a long time to win back.

But however much this was about him, it was also about other men in the congregation who might have the same problem. He could reiterate the percentages. Percentages that said quite a few of these other well-respected men probably accessed porn, but that would not help right now. Each person, each parent or grandparent, was entitled to his or her opinion. He wouldn't fight that. How could he? And many felt betrayed by the pastor for hiring him. The uproar would not go away in a week or even a month—and some would leave.

"I can only assure you that I do not have other computers or phones, and that if Alan sees that I have visited any porn sites, I will be removed from my position immediately."

"That's not good enough." An older man stood. "You should not have been hired, and you should not be allowed to continue."

Jake turned his head, but instead of Alan, John stood and came to the podium. He nudged Jake aside.

"Have a seat," John said under his breath.

The muscles in Jake's shoulders relaxed, and he walked back to John's seat and lowered himself to the chair.

John held up a hand for a moment until the whispering and talking stopped. "I was as surprised as you are when I found out a few days ago about Jake's addiction. And coming from the side of human trafficking, I know how porn is used to groom women and children, to trap men, and to undermine the holiness of godly sexuality. But this is not a war we can afford to ignore. If we are to win it—and we must because it is affecting every layer of our society—then we cannot make men or women afraid to come forward. Do you know how much courage it took for Jake to get up here? If we don't have accountability groups, groups that will educate men and boys in what pornography really does, how it changes the neuro pathways in the brain, how it, in fact, hijacks the male brain and is addictive in the same manner as, say, heroin, then we leave the majority of males, and now even thirty percent of females, without treatment or hope. Is that what we're about?"

Ryann's mom rose. "I understand what you're saying, John, and I feel for Jake and his struggle; but couldn't you take over the youth, and then Jake could lead this group you're talking about?"

"Yeah. That would be good!" someone shouted from the back. Others added their agreement.

John held up his hand again. "You forget I'm leaving soon. Our youth do not need that upheaval in their lives. And Jake feels called—"

"He might feel called, but that doesn't mean that he is."

Ryann stood. "Mom, Jake is a great youth pastor."

Jake caught her smile and smiled back.

Matthew stood beside her. "I agree with Ryann and John and Pastor Alan."

"Well, I don't." The woman in red jumped to her feet again. "I think we need to get a new youth pastor."

Matthew jerked his head around. "How do you know if you got someone else they wouldn't have this same problem? Jake was up front with Pastor Alan. Not everyone is, and who is going to come forward if they know they'll meet this type of opposition?"

"I say we take a vote. This is not a one-man show. We have deacons and elders and all of us. We need to vote on this."

John glanced back at Alan, who stood and came forward. John slipped past him to sit next to Jake.

John leaned over. "You feeling shot?"

Jake forced a smile. "About like that."

"We knew it would be tough."

"Yeah. Just not how tough."

Alan glanced their way, then back toward the congregation. "How many want to vote?" A majority of hands went up.

"Pastor Alan?"

"Yes, China?"

"Can I say something?"

"Of course."

"Many of you know me. You know what kind of person I was when I left here. Talk about addiction. I think I had an addiction to boys and men."

Someone laughed.

"Yeah. Only it wasn't funny. I broke up a number of relationships. I helped with the youth then, and no one stopped me. Maybe they should have. However, the thing was, some of the people I hurt most were the ones who wanted to help me. They thought God could change me. And He has. I came back because I thought God wanted me to, and you know what? Somebody has already offered forgiveness to me. Someone has been praying for me the last couple of years. In fact, more than one person. You could kick me out, too—because in my past I've done a lot I shouldn't have—and maybe I really haven't changed. Maybe I'm just saying that. Just like you're saying about Jake. But God is the God of second chances. He's the God who forgives and gives new life. We can't throw out all those that are hurt and wounded, and we can't deny that when God works in us, it's for real. I say we trust God and give Jake a chance."

Pastor Alan nodded. "Okay. We'll have a vote, but first we'll take a break, and then we'll pray."

>

China went down the steps outside the church. The day had cooled; the night air shifted her short skirt and tugged on her frilly blouse. If the people here didn't want Jake, why would they want her?

"China?"

She stepped off the last step and turned.

Sharee, baby in front carrier, came down the steps. "You're not staying for the vote?"

China shrugged. "Pastor Alan said to take a break. I just wanted to get out of there. I'll be back."

"Okay." Sharee shifted the baby. "Thank you for standing up for Jake. I know this was a surprise to people, but Pastor Alan's right—we have to face the epidemic of porn out there, not pretend it doesn't touch us."

"Makes you wonder if they've ever had problems."

"The other people in there?"

"Yeah."

"You know they have. Some just think the church should be without it, but the church is more a hospital than a resort. They forget."

"Yeah."

"They also forgive."

"Hmm. I wonder."

Sharee touched her arm. "I know this is hard, listening while Jake is attacked, but these people do have children or grandchildren they're worried about. It's a legitimate concern. Jake's truthfulness from the beginning, his steadfastness over the last few years—all those make a case for his staying on as youth pastor."

"I wonder what would happen if they voted on everyone coming into the church. How scary would that be to people? Where would I be?"

"This is not about people coming. It's about someone in leadership. It's different. But China, God's way is whosoever will. He accepts everybody that comes to Him. And you're not just welcome here—you're needed."

"Needed. Right."

"You are. God's done something in your life, and you can share that with others when the time is right. He didn't bring you back here to beat you up. He brought you to be a blessing."

China ducked her head. "I don't know if that will happen."

"Of course it will. Come on. Let's get back inside. Our two votes might be needed."

Chapter 5

Jake leaned back in his chair, raised his arms over his head, and clasped one wrist with his other hand and stretched. Morning light filtered through the pine, oak, and maple trees. The smell of the damp earth around the campsite mixed with the fire's smoke. It was a scent he loved.

God was good.

The vote had gone for him, although not by much, and with restrictions. Ryann's parents would now work with him. But that was okay. He often needed more chaperones than he could round up. The congregation had looked thinner this past Sunday, and the youth group, too. But the first meeting of David's Mighty Men had a larger attendance than they'd expected.

They'd invited those who struggled with pornography and those who wanted to know more about it. In a couple of weeks, they'd separate those two groups and concentrate on those needing help.

He knew their struggle, knew how hard it could be to admit the problem, to take a step to be informed and to begin to change. But something had felt right when he stood up before them to give his testimony.

Thank you for using me to help others, Lord, and for keeping me these last three years. His eyes went to the large tent in which the boys stayed. He knew some of them had already found internet porn sites. The battle started early these days. The internet and pornography were everywhere. *Teach me how to do this, Lord.*

He glanced at Ryann's parents' tent. Once they became more informed about the problem, their help in that area would increase.

The campfire crackled, and he brought his arms down.

The kids had wanted to camp here, even after the alligator incident. He thought he'd have to scratch this place off his list forever. But no, they'd voted, too, and all wanted to come. *Maybe because of the alligator incident.* You never knew.

At any rate, everyone would be able to swim and eat and run, and at night they'd all gather at one campsite and let God do miracles. He always did.

But no alligator stories. Enough was enough, and they'd heard it ad nauseam. Only Ryann still answered questions. China had refused to talk about it at all. Smart girl.

China.

You're doing something in that girl's life, God. Sure wish I knew more about it—and her. He stood, moved to the fire, and picked up the stick he'd leaned against a tree earlier. Better keep the flames going, or the kids would complain.

Kids. Yes. Girl. No.

China wasn't a girl. There was some depth there, some maturity and pain that her quietness hinted at. She was friends with Ryann, making her twenty at the youngest. Probably a year or two older. His twenty-six years felt ancient next to the others. He'd seen too much…

They had set up camp last night, cooked dinner, and sang songs. Some of the youth shared funny stories. They laughed and kidded each other about numerous things. Tonight would be different. He'd asked Ryann and Matthew to give their testimonies. It would be hard and good. He wondered who else God would move on to share.

Smoke rose from the fire, and he scooted to the other side, put the stick down, picked up a few small branches, and set them in the flames.

"So, Mr. Youth Pastor, up early, huh?"

Jake jerked and darted a look to his left.

China grinned at him. Her dark hair was shiny as ever, her eyes dancing in amusement, glad—he could tell—that she'd surprised him. He smiled back, an acknowledgement that she'd caught him off guard.

"It seems I'm not the only early riser." He gave her a quick up and down. She had on a long pair of shorts and a green T-shirt with *Congaree National Park* written across it. She held a small makeup bag in her hand. "Looks like you've been to the bathrooms and back."

"Up early so I don't have to fight for the shower or the sink."

"Ah." He nodded to one of the chairs seated around the fire. "I'll get you some coffee if you want it."

She did a quick lift of her brows. "You make coffee, too?"

"The morning crew—usually me—starts the fire and the coffee."

"Okay. I'll take a cup with one sugar and creamer unless you have some flavored stuff. Then I'll take whatever you have."

He laughed. "Not that choosy then? We have lots of flavored stuff." He moved to the camp stove he'd set up last night, and filled a cup with coffee, then leaned and pulled a carton of flavored creamer from the cooler. After pouring in a generous amount, he handed it to her

She sat in the chair next to his.

"You looking forward to a swim today?"

She sipped the coffee and stared at the fire. "Some. Not a big beach person. I don't swim."

Jake choked on his coffee. "You don't swim?"

"Don't sound so surprised."

"Well, I…" *Hadn't done his research.* Since she'd helped with the youth before, he assumed all requirements had been met. Maybe that wasn't a question on the form. Didn't swim? He couldn't count on her to help there. Well, maybe limited help.

"What? You think because you live in Florida everyone can swim?"

"I…uh…yes, actually. I grew up here. The idea that someone can't swim is foreign."

"And you're on the water all the time with the Coast Guard."

"Yes. And we lose people—children, teens, adults—that can't swim. I assumed…sorry. My fault."

"I make a mean breakfast though."

"Do you? Are you offering to save the girls this morning?"

"Let's say, I'll make sure it's edible."

"What's edible?" Eric slipped into a chair on the other side of China.

"Breakfast."

"That's good to hear. Where'd you get the coffee?"

"Jake made it."

Eric looked past her. "You did? Is it drinkable?"

Jake indicated the camp stove. "Try some."

Eric groaned. "I gotta get it myself?"

"If you want it, dude." Jake did an exaggerated eye roll at China.

She grinned.

Eric shot a glance between them and staggered to his feet. "I'll do this, but only because I'm desperate. Who gets up this early?"

"You do, obviously." The amusement in Jake's voice drew a sour look from Eric.

"Your voices woke me." Eric stumbled to the stove and poured coffee into one of the cups sitting beside it. "Seems like you two spend a lot of time together."

Jake sent a frown China's way. She rounded her eyes and shrugged.

Eric sauntered back and lowered himself into his chair. "Anything we need to know?"

"Dude, you must be still asleep. You're barking up the wrong tree."

"Hmm…just wondered."

China stretched and stood. "Think this is a good time to go wake the girls." She strolled for the tents.

Jake turned his head toward Eric. "What's up with you?"

"Nothing."

"You've been hanging around the girl for weeks, and you come out with that?"

"Just checking the field."

"The field is wide open—if *she*'s agreeable." He pushed himself up and headed back to his tent. "Just make sure she is."

꙳

China stretched her feet toward the campfire and stared at the moonlight filtering through the trees. The day had proved long and challenging, maybe because she recognized how much older she felt than the teens she'd overseen today. The girls seemed so clueless and young—just the way she'd been at one time. She shivered as a cool breeze slipped past the pines and oaks and caused the flames to jump.

The five girls and six boys in the youth group huddled around the fire. Ryann's parents sat off to the side. One of the girls, Carli Sampson, sat close to Jake, a place she'd taken at breakfast and lunch. She delicately ate the last of a gooey treat and looked at Jake from under her long bangs. Jake zipped his jacket and stuffed his hands into his pockets, oblivious to the attention.

China wrapped her arms around herself and stared into the flames. She needed to tell him. Teen girls could develop crushes in a hurry.

Jake had included two other people tonight—

Mitch Houseman, the church's former youth worship leader, and his girlfriend, Jessica Saltare. That had surprised and embarrassed China. She had done her best to seduce Mitch a few years ago. He, like a couple of others, had withstood her charms. China didn't know whether to grimace or grin at the thought. She glanced up to find him watching her and dropped her eyes.

The other guys had fixed hotdogs and hamburgers tonight. Matthew and Eric fought over who knew how to grill best. Besides a little charcoal, they'd both proved pretty respectable cooks.

Most of the group were finishing their s'mores, but something had changed in the atmosphere, almost an expectancy. Matthew cleared his throat and moved forward. His gaze jumped around the circle. One by one the group began to quiet. He put his hand out and gripped Ryann's as she put hers in it.

"Most you know Ryann's story and mine. Well, back a few years ago, John Jergenson came to our youth meeting to talk about purity and abstinence and the sacredness of marriage. He and Sharee were engaged at the time, and they were abstaining from sex—y'all like that word? Abstaining?—anyway, they decided to not have sex until after they married. At the time, a lot of us made fun of them." He glanced at Ryann, then stared into the fire. "A few months before that, Ryann lost her baby. She'd gotten pregnant, and her boyfriend quit youth group and disappeared. So, it was a one-two punch, as they say." He stopped, raised his eyes, and looked around the circle. "She was sixteen. And I—some of you might not know—also had a baby with my girlfriend. I was fifteen. The thing was that I wanted to get married and keep the baby. You know my family. I have six siblings, so one more didn't seem like a big deal. But my girlfriend didn't think so, and neither did her parents. They weren't for us getting married, much less having a baby." He swallowed again.

Ryann leaned forward and rubbed her other hand along his shoulder.

"What happened?" Carli asked.

"She placed the baby for adoption." Deep breath. "I'm so glad she didn't abort it. Thing is, I had no say. She could have done anything, and although it was my baby, too, I had no say. None."

"That's not right."

"Yeah," one of the other guys said. "That's crazy."

"No, it's not." Carli put in. "It's her body."

"It's not her body. It's a baby's body."

"You have no idea…"

Jake held up his hand. "Stop. Okay. We'll do this discussion another time. It's a good one, but right now this is Matthew's testimony and how he felt. Let him finish."

Someone grumbled under their breath, but quiet settled again.

"I still don't know where she is, who her adoptive parents are. Nothing. My girlfriend had a closed adoption. She didn't want me to interfere. You can guess what happened next. We broke up." The fire crackled. A small log fell and sent a light show of sparks into the air. "It took that and watching Ryann go through her…stuff, to see how much she hurt, to make me begin to seek God about sex and marriage. Before it was just…you know, whatever felt good."

He looked around. A few nods met his gaze.

"I'm so glad I now have someone that's come to believe like I do—believes not only that marriage is sacred, but that sex is, too. It's the glue that can hold a marriage together, because it is exclusive to that relationship, not something you do with anyone any time you feel the urge."

A couple of others nodded, one or two said yes, and quiet descended. China leaned back and caught her knee with both hands, wondering if they were nodding in agreement or just to be seen. Whatever. Matthew had come a long way since she'd left two and a half years ago. And if what he said helped even one from this group, then the risk he took opening himself up was worth it.

Mitch Houseman leaned over and picked up his guitar and began to sing.

China kept her focus on Matthew. He pulled Ryann's hand up to his mouth and kissed it.

China's heart squeezed. She'd thrown herself at numerous men. She needed their attention, or so she'd thought. She'd never had her dad's attention. Never would. But looking back, she could only think she needed every other male's attention to prove she was worth something. Funny thing was, as soon as she had their attention, she'd left to find someone new.

Until Tanner.

Talk about seduction. Older by ten years, with money and presence, he'd been totally hot and totally confident about it. Something, in all her so-called sophistication, she'd never met up with before. She fell hard. Whatever he wanted, he got. She'd changed herself in so many ways to please him.

Mitch strummed his guitar, his voice warm and mellow, and the words all about Jesus' love and forgiveness. China sat back and crossed her arms. The night had cooled, but that wasn't the reason. She sang the words with meaning. God had forgiven her. He had swept her up in His love. Tanner had used her and discarded her, but God had loved her.

She caught Jake's studied look and switched her focus to Mitch. Mitch had left to attend college in Tennessee but was home for a weekend—with a girl and a baby. Jessica Saltare. Mitch had introduced her earlier and made sure everyone knew he and Jessica were staying with his parents. He'd introduced her baby, too.

Joy. A cute name. Somehow during the introduction, he'd managed to convey to anyone wondering that, no, it wasn't his baby.

China grinned a little. You had to keep things straight in Christian circles. Still, the girl and Mitch were obviously an item. The baby's father would remain a mystery—for now.

Ryann sat next to Jessica, holding the baby. China contemplated that and wondered what Ryann was thinking. Ryann had been through her own hard time, miscarrying at five months. After what she and Matthew had both been through, no wonder they were waiting to have sex until they married.

Perhaps if her mom had ever sat her down and explained things, or maybe if her dad hadn't left... No, John had tried to talk with her. Even Pastor Alan...

But keeping things straight wasn't just in Christian circles. Tanner had come so often to her apartment in Lexington near the university that some tenants assumed he lived there. He hadn't. He had his own place, but he paid for hers. He hadn't wanted her to be in the dorm. Said she could study better in her own place, and then they could see each other whenever they wanted. Of course, it ended up being whenever he wanted. If she had a final but he wanted to be there, he was. Why had it never bothered her? She was smarter than that.

Mitch's song ended. The anointing, the feel of God's presence, hung over the group.

Her heart beat hard against her chest, and she tried to swallow the words that suddenly pushed against her throat. She coughed.

Jake leaned forward. His focus moved from the fire to her. "You have something to share, China?" His voice had dropped from its usual level and softened.

No. But her heart stroked hard against her chest, and an invisible hand pressed her back.

"Uh. No."

Jake nodded but said nothing. No one else spoke. *God, I don't want to share this, to share anything.* Silence met her. Matthew's eyes caught hers. She glanced down. The fire sputtered. Sparks fanned upward, dancing.

She cleared her throat. "Well, maybe...if it will help someone."

Jake nodded again, said nothing again.

China stared at the glowing logs. "Two years ago, I left here to go to college. I couldn't believe my luck. Getting away from home—and from the church." She hesitated and found Ryann's gaze, then Mitch's. "I felt hemmed in here. I was crazy about guys, and the harder they were to get, the more I liked them. If they had a girlfriend, well, cheez, I'd go after him even more." She dropped her eyes. "I wasn't into wrecking marriages, but anyone else was fair game. I...I knew what I was doing was wrong, but I still went after every guy I could. I ruined as many relationships as I could. Some, though, I couldn't."

She cleared her throat, waiting a moment as the fire shot upward with another breeze. "I moved to Kentucky and took out loans and went to college. I did good at first, but then, you know, partying and dating took their toll. I worked, too. Waitressing. An older guy began to come by each night. I say older—you know, ten years or so older. Hot and with a lot of money. His name was Tanner. He asked me out finally, and I went. Wow. He took me places that I'd never been to, bought me stuff, sent me stuff at the dorm and at work. I...loved it, loved the attention and him." The breeze fingered its way through the campsites again. She brought her head up. "You know how that is?"

Heads bobbed up and down.

"Yeah. Well, I had never cared for anyone before, and when he said he wanted me to move off campus, get an apartment so we could...be together...whenever we wanted, well, I agreed." She swallowed. How could she tell everyone this? Let them know what she was? She stared into the orange flames. "He paid for the apartment. Said he was helping with my education. He asked me to quit my job, said he would make up the income; and I could study more, bring my grades up, and we could be together." The quiet intensified, almost as if she could hear their concentration. "I never thought about it. I mean, how great to have someone give me an apartment and money so I could study…" Her voice trailed off.

One of the guys snickered.

"Shut up, Eric." Jake's voice was low but pointed.

China glanced at him. His eyes met hers. She ducked her head. "Yeah. You all see where this is going. I…I was kept by him. I didn't think of it that way. I really thought I loved him and that he loved me. Until I got sick." The ache in her heart started again. She brought a fist to her mouth. "I…I got really sick. The doctors thought I might need surgery."

Ryann's gasp startled her. "You…you never called."

"I know. I…I couldn't. He…he kicked me out."

"*What?*" Ryann's voice jumped.

Mitch said something under his breath, and others stirred.

"I…I couldn't be what he wanted if I was sick, if I had surgery. He told me I needed to come home to mom and to the church." She forced a laugh. "I'd run away from that, and now when I needed someone, he told me to go back. The funny thing was, it was like the devil and God telling me the same thing—Tanner being the devil."

Ryann handed the baby back to Jessica. "But what surgery? Are you okay now?"

"Yes. This was almost a year ago. I…I didn't come back, although I guess I should have. I spent some time after the surgery getting my life turned around."

"And now you're back," Jake said.

China met Jake's look again. "Yes."

He smiled. "Finally doing what God wanted?"

She smiled, too. "Yes, I guess I am. Running from God didn't help."

"Never does."

Ryann scooted up next to her and threw her arms around her. "I can't believe you didn't call me."

China held tight to her, fighting the pain in her throat and the tears in her eyes. Mitch strummed his guitar and began to sing quietly. Another of the girls moved and sat next to China. They all began to sing.

Chapter 6

The morning air's coolness drove Jake to the fire pit. He rubbed his hands together, picked up the stick he used for a poker, and stirred the ashes. No spark there. He grabbed some wood they'd gathered yesterday and began to build another fire. As he put paper and dry leaves down, a few students climbed from their tents and headed to the bathroom. He smiled as Ryann stumbled over a root in her path, then continued on. Her long, straight hair looked cobwebbed and mussed. China, Jessica, and another girl followed.

He put small twigs on top of the paper and leaves and glanced up. China grimaced at him, and he smiled. Her black hair was pulled back in a ponytail, and she wore a pair of flannels and a T-shirt and staggered after the other girls. He'd missed her this morning, but her testimony last night had enough emotional hooks in it to keep her in bed awhile longer today. He understood that. She might not want a tête-à-tête with him or anyone else right now.

Jake stacked the larger sticks over the other material, teepee fashion, then lit the paper and leaves and watched as it caught the kindling above it. He moved back and sat in his chair, enjoying the sight and the smell as the yellow-orange flame jumped and leapt and grew.

He heard the girls laughing and talking before he could see them. Eric, Mitch, and Matthew had risen and made it to the bathrooms and back before the girls had. He watched as all his male campers straightened and looked toward the giggling. Spring was definitely in the air—and heavy with hormones.

The girls had breakfast duty again, and as they filed into the camp, they all headed for the camp stove and food he'd set nearby. Most sported wet hair, makeup, and clean clothes. China appeared last, her hair dry and combed, as if she'd never slept on it. But he drew in a breath as she passed his Jeep and came into full view.

She had on a simple T-shirt. This one with *Amicalola Falls State Park* stamped on it. His attention, though, focused on her shorts and the raven tattoo that showed on her thigh. He jumped from the chair, spun around, and walked away.

Every time he thought about the tattoo, he had to forcibly thrust it from his mind. The sight of it was like a key to his past, a key he did not want and would not use. China hadn't worn anything to show it off since that first day, and he'd begun to relax. Dumb move.

He stopped at his Jeep and went through the items left in the back. Nothing he needed here except time.

"You want coffee?" China thrust a cup in front of him.

He took the cup and took a sip but didn't look around. "Thanks." He set the cup on the bumper and pulled another box toward him.

"You looking for something special?"

Why didn't she leave? Go talk to someone else? A thousand answers went through his mind, but none would make sense.

He blew out a breath. "No. I'm avoiding you."

She didn't say anything right away, but a moment later when he still hadn't looked her way, she said, "I'm not sure if you're joking or if you're serious."

He straightened and turned her way. Anger fingered up his spine. Anger at her and the shorts and the tattoo. "I'm serious." He forced himself to look at her, knowing the anger showed whether he wanted it to or not.

"Oh." Uncertainty wavered, but she nodded and

turned. "All right." The words were low.

He caught her arm, but she shook free. "Look, why did you wear the shorts this morning?"

"What?"

"The shorts. They show your tattoo."

"So what?"

He gritted his teeth. "Thanks for the coffee, but…" He backed up from the Jeep. His eyes dropped to the tattoo as if they were heat-seeking missiles. He snapped them shut, whirled, and walked off.

The noise in his head shook him, and he lengthened his stride. The next moment, he was jogging. Good. That was what he needed. Sunlight spilled through the trees, creating light and shade along the path. He continued to run. She'd worn long pants or long shorts until this morning. He hadn't been ready for it. Not that he would ever be. He shook his head. No, he'd come through that. He could handle this. He'd told Alan this wasn't a problem.

His pace slowed. Why had she gotten that tattoo? Could she possibly know? The first time he'd seen her, he thought she must, but now he wasn't so sure.

He turned and began to walk back. Okay, he would handle this. He'd take half the group swimming. Those who didn't want to swim, or couldn't—and that included China—he'd have Matt or Mitch take them on a hike. And by the time they met again for lunch, he'd have another plan for the afternoon.

Night brought cooler temperatures, and China changed to jeans and a pullover shirt with a hoodie. She'd purposely worn the shorts all day. If they were such a problem, then he could just say so. She shrugged. They were short. There was probably some kind of rule about how long shorts had to be. Just like the girls had to wear T-shirts over their bathing suits. She didn't think it mattered once they were wet, but someone had made the rule.

Jake had managed to stay away from her all day, and as the hours passed, her anger climbed.

What was his problem? His actions today mirrored those of the first day she'd returned to church. Only then, she had no idea why he'd run. Today she still wasn't sure. The shorts or the tattoo? Quite a few of the youth had tattoos, so how could that cause trouble?

Mitch led the praise and worship again, but Jake rushed the campfire time. He didn't wait for testimonies or sharing. Instead, he encouraged everyone to turn in early. They needed to pack and head home tomorrow morning.

As the others slipped away or took moonlit walks, she cornered him, moving between the fire and his Jeep.

He glanced at her and dipped his head. "Yes?"

Her hands went to her hips. "If my shorts were a problem, you should have said something."

"The shorts are too short, especially for a chaperone, but that's not the problem."

"Well, the tattoo shouldn't be. Lots of Christians have—"

"It's a problem. I'd appreciate it if you kept it covered from now on."

She huffed. "You really are being a snoot about this."

"I'm sorry, but I…"

"Sorry? You don't sound sorry. You just sound angry and…and bigoted." Her throat had tightened again. She threw up her hands and turned.

He caught her arm. "I'm not bigoted. Just keep it covered, will you?"

"You know what? It's not a problem. You're the problem."

"It is a problem—when it's a porn star's signature."

Everything in her stilled. "What?"

Jake glanced toward the fire and the tents and lowered his voice. "Twila James. Porn star. That is her signature tattoo."

China couldn't say a word. A porn star's tattoo? Tanner had insisted she get it. She'd given in to keep him happy. Her chest contracted, but a moment later a volcano shot up inside her. *The sleazebag.* The absolute sleazebag. How could he?

"Is it in the same place?"

Jake nodded.

She couldn't look at him. The life she'd lived then… The things she'd done for Tanner—a lot more than a tattoo.

She met Jake's frown. What was he thinking? "You…how do you…"

His face tensed. "You know how I know."

The words were low, balanced, steady, but his look reflected something else. Shame?

She swallowed. If it was, the same emotion gripped her. Along with the lava building inside, ready to spew forth. If she could get her hands on Tanner Larson. "I can't believe this."

Jake looked past her for a moment and cleared his throat.

China's gaze fell. How could she say anything when she'd sold herself for an apartment, for money to go to college, for nice dinners and the feeling of being loved? "I need to be alone."

A cloud covered the moon, and the shadows grew around them. "All right."

Something in his voice halted her a second, but the ache in her heart turned her; and she headed past him.

"Don't go far."

She shrugged. Who cared how far she went? In fact, the farther, the better. Maybe she could get away from the pain. She'd thought Tanner just grew into a jerk.

He couldn't possibly have been like that when they started dating, but he'd been that way from the start.

"Don't go far. Don't get lost. It's dark out here." Jake's voice, concerned. *Right.* Getting lost seemed like a good thing to do right now.

"China."

She waved a hand at him and walked out of the flickering firelight into the dark.

She swallowed the pain in her throat. After the first time, Tanner began to press her about the tattoo. *That early in their relationship.* And he'd started buying her clothes, urging her to wear them when they went out or were in the apartment.

She whirled and walked back to where Jake still stood. "Do I look like her?" She tried to keep her voice level, but it hadn't worked. "This...this porn star. Do I look like her?"

"Not your face."

"But? I hear the *but.*"

"Your...body type, your hair."

She swallowed, twirled, and strode into the night again, thoughts and pain buzzing in her head like a swarm of bees. Oh, Lord, Tanner *was* a creep from day one. He'd picked her out of a crowd because she reminded him of a porn star, and then he'd dressed her and used her.

You are new in Christ.

I'm not new. How can I ever be new? Tanner had acted like she had the plague when she told him about the surgery.

She'd come right from the doctor's office to find him. "The doctor said I need to do it as soon as possible."

Silence. He'd stepped away. "You're not expecting me to be there, right?"

"What? Of course I am. Just be there. I need someone."

"What about your mother? Your friends? Or that

church you used to go to? They're the type of people you want."

Pain and confusion still stampeded inside. How could this happen to her? "I don't want them. I want you."

"I'm not good at this type of stuff."

"No one is 'good' at it. You just do it."

He shifted backward, away from her. "I don't do it. I don't do sickness. I like things that look good, smell good. And this relationship is all about the sex. You know that. It has been from day one."

She stumbled over the roots in the path, tears blinding her. Moonlight flitted again through the trees, giving some light to the trail, but it didn't matter.

And it hadn't mattered then, not after Tanner's words sunk in, after he'd grudgingly given her permission to stay in the apartment until she'd recovered from her surgery. That conversation, on top of the doctor's diagnosis, had caused a slide into darkness that lasted for months.

Until the day the lady in the clinic began to talk about God and Jesus, about healing and forgiveness. Not that China had wanted to hear it. Anger at God and Tanner filled her. Despair ripped her heart. But after that first day, the lady was always there. China used to groan when she saw her. If God existed, how had He allowed this to happen to her?

She'd yelled at God back then. "How could you do this to me? Are you punishing me?"

If not for the woman in the chair continuing to tell her of God's love, of His goodness, of how He made all things new, she night never have come out of it. On the woman's last day, she handed China a book and a note, a note China still cherished. It said that China was precious in God's sight, that He would never leave her, and in exchange for all the horror and pain she'd been through, God would give her something good.

China stumbled over another root and fell into a tree. Pain shot through her shoulder. She gasped, drew back, and pounded the tree's trunk—the ache in her fist echoing that in her heart. Tears welled up and spilled down her cheeks. *I thought you healed me of this, God. Where are you tonight?*

Above, the stars sat cold against the dusky sky. She lowered her head, brushed her hands off on the jeans, and wiped the tears from her face. The wind caused the shadows to shift and change around her. She and God had dealt with her pain and her sin over this last year. She'd spent days and weeks in a pop-up tent in numerous state or national parks, seeking Him, seeking the healing she needed. And she'd found it, or thought she had.

You are new in Christ.

Am I? She rubbed the tears from her face again, then stamped her foot. She'd run. The enemy had accused her once again, and she'd run. The shame of her past life had overflowed. *But I am a new creature in Christ. That is true. It has to be true, or I'm nothing.* She straightened. *God's Word has to be true.*

She turned and headed back.

The path twisted and darkened. The moonlight disappeared. Ahead, the trees bent and covered the way she should go. She stopped and squinted into the night. Another path led to the right. Uncertainty ran a cold finger up her spine. Had she seen this path before? Which way should she go? Wind whipped her hair and cooled her arms.

The strength of a minute ago left. *Lord? Where am I?*

Something moved in the bushes near her, and she jumped. Moonlight flooded the trail again. To her left, a small rodent scurried across the path and through the brush. She stepped back, and her foot caught on a ropelike root. She stumbled, tried to turn, to catch herself…and fell.

❧

So, she hadn't known about the tattoo.

Shadows raced along the moonlit ground, and Jake gazed down the path she'd taken. Everyone else was in camp, most huddled in their tents, talking, but China hadn't returned.

No, she hadn't known about the tattoo, but the guy had. Obviously. He must have talked her into getting it somehow.

He zipped his jacket higher. The night had cooled. Where was she? She'd acted over the top when he told her about the tattoo. Not what he'd expected—if, that was, he'd expected anything. He stood, ambled to the fire, grabbed the stick, and stirred it. No, he hadn't thought about it. He'd just blurted out what had bothered him and let it fall.

"You coming to bed tonight, J.T.?" Mitch stepped beside him, staring at the flames. "If so, you might want to let that fire die."

Jake nodded, his mind going back over the conversation he'd had with China. He winced. He'd ignored the cues she'd given, the ones that said she was hurt—bad. "Look, do you mind watching this? Or putting it out? I need to find China."

"She's not in the tent with the others?"

"Not unless she slipped past me."

"Let me ask Ryann and Jessica."

"Okay. Check it out." He leaned over to the camp chair and pulled a flashlight from the cup holder. Yeah, maybe she had come back and snuck past him somehow, but he didn't think so.

Mitch straightened from the tent doorway. "Nope. She's not inside. They haven't seen her for a while."

"*Great*. Look, I'll go find her. I know the paths around here. Mind staying up in case she comes back?"

Mitch strolled back his way. "No prob. I'll sit

here by the fire and wait for you both. Don't you get lost."

"Not planning on it, but she might be—lost, that is. It's dark, and she didn't take a light. But if she stayed on the trail, I'll find her." He turned and headed down the path she'd taken. Didn't he tell her not to get lost?

The light illuminated the path before him, and some of the brush on either side. What if she'd tripped over some of the roots intertwining the path? She could be lying somewhere with a broken ankle. Nah. The woman seemed pretty tough.

A little farther from the camp, and he called her name. Not shouting. Other campers were around, but most were back past where their group had set up. If she looked, she'd see his flashlight from a distance.

Okay, God, please help me find her.

He flashed the light up the path through the trees and on each side. If she saw it, surely she'd come toward him. The moonlight was bright even without the flash, but the light thrust into the darkness like a beacon.

How far would she go? He knew a smaller path broke off from the main one not far ahead. It was almost hidden coming from this way, especially at night. But coming back, she might see it, get confused, and take it. He picked up his pace.

"China."

Her name seemed to echo, and he listened. Nothing. The breeze kicked up, and the chill went through his jacket. Away from the fire, the cold penetrated his clothing. What was she wearing? Pants and some type of hoodie thing. Nothing warm.

"China." He flashed the light through the trees again. Now the wind was moaning, and he couldn't hear over it. "China!"

The moaning sounded nearer, and he spun around, throwing his light into the trees and shrubs. "China?"

"Ja...ke."

His flash caught a jean-covered leg first, and then her body sprawled in the bushes right off the path. When it touched her face, she blanched and covered her eyes.

He scrambled off the path and knelt next to her. "Hey, girl, you okay?"

"I…I don't know. A rat ran by me, and I jumped and fell. But I didn't want to move. Something seems to be sticking in my back."

He shifted the light, playing it down her body and back. "Where does it hurt?"

"Everywhere. I landed so hard, and there's a thousand things sticking in me."

He hadn't seen any blood, but he couldn't see the side next to the ground.

"Hmm. Hold this." He handed her the light and slipped a hand under her. Sure enough, a hard round object was directly beneath her. "Yep, a rock or something. Hard, but not sharp. Did you twist anything? Your ankle? Let me check that." He moved his hands down to her feet and ankles and gingerly squeezed them. "This okay?"

"Yes."

"All right. Try to sit up, and then we'll get you to the path and see how you are." When he tugged on her arm, she rose to a sitting position. He moved and slipped his arm around her waist. "Come on. To your feet."

She groaned but stood. When she wobbled, he tightened his grip. They stepped to the path, and he took the flashlight from her hand.

"Let me look." He held her as he waved the light like an airport security wand. Something had gouged small tears along her arms and in the fabric of her top. He pressed against those. She jumped. "I guess that hurts."

Her head came up. "I guess you're right."

"But I don't see any blood. I'd say you're okay."

She pulled free of his arm and tugged down on her hair. "Clever deduction, Nancy Drew."

For a moment, he missed her warmth and the feel of her body next to his. "I'm sure there is some guy you could compare me to."

"If I think of one, I'll let you know."

He grinned and shook his head. "Well, come on. Can you can walk?"

"Sure."

In spite of the toughness in her voice, she took a hesitant step. He put a hand under her elbow, and when she'd taken three more, he tightened his hold.

"Hey," she said and tried to pull free. "Let go. I'm fine."

"Except you're going the wrong way."

"What? Oh…"

He chuckled. "Good thing I'm looking out for you."

"I guess."

He remained quiet, and a moment later, she added, "Thank you for coming to look for me."

"No prob. I didn't want a search party unless we needed it."

"That would have been embarrassing."

"Make sure you check everything when we get back to camp. Go to the bathroom and wash any scratches and put some antibiotic cream on them."

"My goodness. Yes, Granny."

He hadn't let go of her arm, and now gave her a tough squeeze. She yanked free.

"And if any of them need stitches, come tell me."

"Yes, Granny."

"Any more of that and I'll pick you up before we get to camp and carry you in."

"What? Why?"

"I'm sure the girls are still up, waiting for you. If I carry you in, everyone will pour out of the tents wanting to know what's wrong. I'm sure I can think of a tall tale to interest them."

She slapped his arm. "Nothing could get taller than the alligator."

He nodded but said nothing.

"Sorry. Not funny."

"No, but probably true."

They walked in silence, China limping slightly. When the fire's orange glow appeared, he clicked off his flashlight.

"Ah. Home." China's steps quickened.

Mitch's head rose when they strode into the firelight. Jessica sat next to him, curled against his side. "You're back. Everything okay?"

A pang of envy went through him. It had been two years since his last relationship. A long time.

"Yeah. Except for some scrapes and bruises." He glanced at China as she stopped in front of the fire and smiled. She rubbed her hands up and down her arms. Yep. Cold. He'd known it. That hoodie thing was more style than warmth.

Ryann appeared from the girls' tent. "You okay, China? We were waiting on you."

"Yeah, I'm okay. I fell into some bushes. Jake helped me back."

Ryann stepped closer. "You're sure you're okay?"

"Yeah, but I might need some help doctoring a few scrapes."

"I'll get the first-aid kit. Get your stuff, and we'll head to the bathhouse."

China glanced up at him, and he noticed her swollen eyes. His chest tightened. He reached out and touched her shoulder, but she turned away. As she limped toward the tent, anger at a man he'd never met spread a fire inside him.

Chapter 7

Jake grinned at China as she climbed into the Jeep. "A good day."

"Yeah. I didn't think we'd get that whole room done today."

"You didn't think twelve kids could knock out one youth room?"

"That was the reason. Twelve kids in one room with all that paint? I thought it would look like a paintball field by the time we finished."

Jake lifted a hand from the wheel. "You do paintball?"

"Before I left for college, I was a pro."

"Oh, you were? Is that a challenge?"

"Only if you think you can take me."

He lowered his head and sent her a narrow-eyed look. "That's a challenge."

She laughed. "We'll see if you're up to it. The others would love it, too."

"The next calendar event then."

"You plan it. I'll be there."

"It's on. Prepare to get walloped."

"Ha! You better prepare for defeat."

He chuckled, then sobered. "Interesting what Ryann said."

"The Gideon three hundred?"

"I guess they feel like that."

"Don't feel bad about it. It will make us all closer."

"Some of their friends have left, and that's my fault."

"They have, but new friendships will form."

Jake said nothing. The girl seemed to have gotten her feet back under her after the camping trip last weekend, and she did well with the youth. Especially… "Nice save, by the way."

"What? Oh, Becky." Her eyes lit.

"When Chance knocked her ladder over, we all freaked."

"And the look on Becky's face. I didn't know if I should grab her or the ladder." China turned in her seat. "For one second I thought if I held on to the ladder, maybe she could regain her balance."

"It was hypnotic, watching her fall. John and I were too far away. You get this empty feeling in the pit of your stomach, knowing you can't make it there in time."

"You mean the big, bad Coast Guard man had no idea how to help?"

He grinned. "Yes, ma'am, that's exactly what I mean."

Her amusement was obvious. She liked being able to outdo him. He'd have to remember that. She had a competitive streak.

"I'm sorry you had to bring me home." Her voice jolted him back.

"I said I would."

"I can't believe Eric ran out on me."

"On the group. But that's not much of a surprise. At least he came. We had a number that didn't show at all. But if you're thinking about going out with the guy, just realize he's…not always reliable."

"I think I've noticed that before. When he decided to leave today, he didn't ask what I thought or needed. Just said he was leaving."

Jake nodded. That was one worry off his mind. He hadn't brought himself to the point of trying to give a warning about Eric, hadn't decided whether he should or not. She gave another direction and then pointed out her house. Renting, she'd told him. Cheaper than an apartment or condo, and she liked the privacy.

"Right there. Thanks again."

He pulled into the drive, shut off the engine, and climbed from the Jeep. "I'll help you carry this stuff inside."

"Oh. Okay."

He handed her the short ladder and picked up a box of paint supplies. "These were a big help."

"Well, I'd just painted this place, so I had everything on hand."

"And you didn't want help when you had painting to do?"

"No. I mean, Mom offered, but she's worked overtime ever since dad left. She didn't need to spend a weekend helping me. It was just easier to do it myself."

"The youth would have helped." When she only nodded, he followed her to the front door. "How long's your dad been gone?"

"About twelve years. He just left one day. Took the car and his clothes. We've never heard from him since."

Jake winced. "That's hard."

"It was."

She shifted the ladder to the other hand and pulled her keys from a pocket of her shorts. Long shorts. A loose T-shirt. Why she didn't wear something as unprovocative to church, he didn't understand. Tight shirts and even tighter pants still had him looking away—and other guys watching the doors for her. No cleavage though. At least she was modest on that account.

She threw open the door and pointed to the table in the kitchen. He walked through the living area and set the box down.

"Nice place."

"I like it." She lifted both hands. "I got to decorate

just the way I wanted for a change. It was fun."

"You like green." His gaze took in the greens and
sand colors and occasional white in the sofa, barrel
chairs, area rugs, and accessories. The wooden floors
added warmth. Her walls had a few large paintings,
mostly scenes from state parks. Their names were
blazoned across them.

"Yeah. It reminds me of the outdoors."

He stepped close to one of the paintings. "You
really do like camping and hiking then?"

"I didn't, but this last year, well, things changed. I
do now."

He slipped his hands into the pockets of his jeans,
tilted his head, and looked at her. "So, is it your escape?"

She turned and set the ladder down, then reached
up and tugged on her hair. "In a way."

He was quiet for a moment but then turned and
headed for the door. "Now all you need is to learn to
swim."

"One day."

"I'll teach you. I have a boat. We'll go out to one
of the islands, and you can learn. It's easy once you get
past the fear."

"I don't know…"

"Easy." He tilted his head. "Unless you're
chicken." Her eyes narrowed, and he grinned. "Chicken."

"Okay. You're on."

He smirked. Now that he knew that competitive
streak hid just under her skin, he'd have some fun.
"Good. Two things to put on the calendar."

"Do it."

He turned when he got to the door and cleared his
throat. "Your outfit looks nice today. Modest clothes in
church would go a long way in having others accept
you." When her face changed, he felt the twinge of guilt.
"All right. I'm out of here."

He closed the door behind him but stopped. Why

had he said that? No, he knew why—because even though it might be true with others, it was definitely true with him. On Sundays, he stayed as far away from her as he could. But that was his problem. Yes, the way she dressed added to it, but he didn't need to guilt her.

He rapped on her door, twisted the handle, and pushed it open. "Look, I'm sorry about that last remark. I—"

She had tilted her head sideways, grabbed the top of her hair, and was pulling it off. Something jolted inside him. He stared, even as she did. The long, black hair now hung from her hand. Her own head was covered with about two or three inches of fine blond hair. He swallowed. In fact, in the light from the kitchen window behind her, she looked almost bald.

Her eyes were wide, and her gaze went between the black hair she held in her hand and him. She cringed. "What are you doing?" Her voice was high.

He struggled to find his. "I was just—"

"Get out of here! Get out!"

"I—"

"Get out!"

He slammed the door and stood on the outside again, surprise rocketing through him. *Her hair was a wig.* In fact, she had no hair—or very little. She looked so different, so…childlike.

Sounds reached him from inside the house. Something slammed against the wall. He took a step away, dug his keys from his pocket, and stopped again. Words rose, as if she was railing against someone, then tear-filled words, then sobs.

He flinched.

Lord, what do I do?

He received no answer, and he slowly walked back to his Jeep. He waited for a few more minutes, his heart confused, but then he backed out and headed home.

She was bald.

Well…almost.

Tomorrow was Sunday. He'd see her then, and when he did, what would he say?

❧

He stepped from the shower and rubbed his head with the towel. Why would she shave her head? It made no sense. He'd seen her tug on her hair numerous times, but it never made it through his thick skull that she had a wig. He finished toweling off.

Maybe she hadn't shaved her head, but if she hadn't… Chemotherapy would cause her hair to *fall* out. He knew that. His grandmother had cancer. But that was ridiculous. China was too young.

He slipped on a pair of shorts and headed to the kitchen. So maybe he should call, but the sound of her sobbing filled him. Women and tears had never been his forte.

Then why are you a youth pastor, Osborne? He yanked meat, cheese, and mustard from the refrigerator and glanced around for the bread. If it were any of the youth, he'd plan on doing or saying something. He'd plan his next step. It was just…he couldn't plan right now. He kept seeing her face and the wig in her hand.

Slapping the sandwich together and pulling a bag of chips from the cupboard, he headed for the kitchen table. Maybe she had shaved it. For some reason. The possibility danced inside his head. Better than the alternative. He'd chewed through half the sandwich before he let the next thought enter.

She might not come to church tomorrow.

She didn't.

❧

She hadn't answered his phone calls either until he called so early Monday morning that she must have grabbed it without thinking.

"Hello?" Her voice was a growl.

"Meet me at Starbucks near your place in thirty minutes," he said.

"What?"

"Starbucks in thirty minutes. I'm buying. Bring your appetite."

"I'm not awake."

"That's what Starbucks is for. See you in thirty."

"Wait. I don't know. I—"

He hung up and went to throw on his clothes. When he drove up, her car was already there. He parked the Jeep and went inside.

She had on the black wig, but his quick glance took in more than that. She wore black shorts, very short shorts, showing the tattoo. She'd topped the shorts with a white blouse, black running bra underneath. Not that she'd tried to hide that. The coffee in this place wasn't as hot as she was. She'd obviously worn the outfit on purpose—just to get to him. She didn't want to talk and wasn't going to make it easy.

He should walk out. Just walk out.

Every male eye in the place followed her as she stepped up next to him. He nixed everything he wanted to say. Instead, he said nothing.

She moved her head back. "You want to talk?" The words challenged.

All right. They still needed the conversation, but… "Yeah, we need to talk, but I'm not talking with you like that."

"Like what?"

The heat of anger went through him, and he raked his eyes down her and back up. "Dressed like that. Don't you have modest clothes?"

Her eyes narrowed. "You said that Saturday, too. What have my clothes got to do with this?"

"For one thing, I thought we'd have a private conversation, but you have every Joe-shmo in here salivating over you."

Her mouth flat-lined. "It's not my fault if they have a problem with my outfit."

"Yeah, well, I have a problem with it. And you're right—it's not your problem. It's mine. So, I'm out of here." He stepped past her and headed toward the door. She'd looked good Saturday, and they'd worked out some sort of friendship, or so he thought, but it would never go anywhere like this.

When he shoved open the door, he realized she was right behind him.

"Wait up, Joe-shmo. I want to finish this."

He walked away from the door and let his eyes take in the parking lot. "There's nothing to finish."

"Oh yes, there is. You call me to meet you here because you have something important to say, or think you have something important to say, and now you run out. What is this?"

"It's me with a problem."

"So get over it. Get past it. I know I don't dress like all the girls at church, but this is how I dress—sometimes."

"Yeah, and that's the problem."

"What? You won't talk to me unless I dress the way you like? You know, I thought you might be different from Tanner, but you're not. Everything has to be your way, doesn't it?"

"You have no idea what you're talking about."

She shoved her face close to his. "I know exactly what I'm talking about. I got thrown aside by another jerk who wanted to run my life, to tell me what to wear, when to wear it, and when he had time for me. In fact, this is the kind of outfit he liked. I just grabbed something this morning. Sorry if it doesn't meet your qualifications."

Her voice sputtered, anger rising to match his—only his had the air slowly seeping from it. Words strangled in his throat. Hurt and angst mixed with the anger in her voice, and he heard it.

Her eyes were slits. "You know what? I don't need any of this from you or anyone else. Have a great day."

He caught her arm as she whirled away, and she snatched it free. "Let go of me!"

"Wait a minute."

"Not a chance."

He followed her to her car. "All right. You had your say. Let me have mine."

She fumbled to open the door, and he took advantage of that and leaned into her space. "Don't put me in the same class as this Tanner guy. That guy used you. I wouldn't do that. But I have a problem. You know it. It's mine, but your outfit aggravates it."

She said nothing. Her face was averted, and he couldn't see it.

"Did you hear that?"

"No." She managed to get the door open and slid into the driver's seat.

Her voice had broken on the one word. Was she crying? "China—"

"Look, pretty lady, is this guy bothering you?"

Jake jerked upright and stared at two guys standing behind him.

"You bothering the lady, maverick?"

The guy had about the same height and weight on him that Jake did, but his friend hit six feet or more and carried a good fifty pounds extra. The first man's words held a threat.

Maverick? Jake straightened and settled his shoulders, eyeing them. Great. Two good ole boys looking for a fight.

"What?" China's voice sounded surprised.

"If this guy's bothering you, we can take care of him."

Jake wanted to shake his head. It was Starbucks

and daylight, not a bar at two in the morning. He bit back the "Get lost" he wanted to say. No sense aggravating the situation.

China pushed from the car and stood beside him. "Nah, I'm fine." She slid an arm around Jake's waist. "We always go on like this. It doesn't mean anything."

Both men's eyes slid from China's face to Jake's. Neither looked pleased.

"Really, we're fine." China's voice took on a southern accent. "But I appreciate you boys. I'll just remind him of this if he gets out of line."

Jake shot her a glance. She did that southern-charm thing well. He took her lead, slipped his arm around her shoulders, then focused back on the other two men.

The man closest to him stepped forward, his eyes dark and narrowed.

The taller man put a hand on his shoulder. "Come on, Billy. Leave them alone. The girl said she's okay."

"I just want to know I'm getting the truth."

"I 'preciate that, Billy." China's voice still held its charm. "I really do, but I'm okay. Jake wouldn't hurt a fly—unless it's a horsefly, of course."

Billy made a noise in his throat. "Well, if you need us, we'll be right inside." His head indicated the coffee shop. With another scowl at Jake, he turned and walked past his buddy. The taller man gave Jake a matching scowl but nodded toward China and followed Billy inside.

Jake waited until they disappeared before removing his arm from her shoulders. "I think you just saved me from getting pounded."

She took a step back. "Yeah, well, it would have been my fault—somewhat—if you got pounded."

Neither said anything for a moment. Then Jake cleared his throat. "Look, when I said it was my problem, I meant it." He chewed his lip. Maybe he hadn't said enough to give her an idea of the struggle he'd had. "But there's a lot more to this than I said."

"Yeah?" Her tone still held its belligerence. "Tell me."

He put a hand against the car and glanced around the parking lot. Not something he wanted to share in a public place. He sighed. "A neighbor introduced me to porn when I was eleven. I knew it was wrong, but it didn't make much difference until I came to know Christ. And then I struggled for years."

"Yeah."

She wasn't making this easy. "Porn's addictive. It changes your brain. And it can ruin relationships, both emotionally and physically. Of course, it's sexually stimulating, and that's a great escape when things go wrong, especially if you're a guy."

Her brow furrowed. "An escape? Sure."

"Look, it's an addiction, something to run to when…when you don't want to deal with or think about things." He shifted and leaned against the car. "I'm not proud of this. I used it if I was depressed or guilty. You get a kind of high and a sense of control—for a short time." He hesitated. "In that sense, it's a lot like drugs—heroin, alcohol. I had to learn to lean on Christ, not…something else. And then I had to fight the desire that goes with it. Not an easy fix. But I got free. I am free."

She crossed her arms, her look searching his. "So today…"

"When you walked into church a month ago, well… The tattoo blew my mind. I've done a lot of battling since. And today…" He swallowed. "It's a problem."

"So you're saying…" She glanced down at her clothes.

"Talking with you right now is hard."

"Okay." She pushed past him, went to the trunk,

and opened it. A moment later, she held up a pair of
sweat pants and a T-shirt. "Let me change, and we can
talk."

❧

Starbucks and the good ole boys disappeared from
her rearview mirror, and she followed him to Fred
Howard Park. Spanish moss waved in the large oaks as
they parked near one of the shelters. The cool wind slid
along her arms. Maybe she should have left him in the
parking lot, too.

She sighed. She knew when she threw the outfit
on that he wouldn't like it, but she hadn't thought about
causing any real problem. She'd worn it to aggravate
him, just as she was aggravated—and not wanting to
discuss the topic he had on his mind. *That was her
problem.* Wanting to keep her secret. She blew out a long
breath. She'd been proud of her body once, and now...

She turned and watched him climb from the Jeep.
At least he admitted to his problem. Could she talk about
hers? She crossed her arms over her chest.

"You want to walk?"

Jake's voice held a conciliatory tone, but she still
wasn't happy. "No. Actually, I don't know why I'm here
or why I let you con me into meeting you in the first
place."

His mouth hitched. "You came because you were
still asleep and coffee beckoned. The rest is just
circumstance."

She narrowed her eyes. "You can do that amusing
thing all you want, but I don't have to talk to you."

"No, you don't." He indicated the path in front of
them. "Let's walk anyway."

She moved past him, and he fell in step beside
her. What was she doing? She should just climb back into
her car and leave. She shook her head.

"What?"

"Nothing."

He slid a glance her way. "Okay. Let's jog a
little." He caught her arm and pulled her into a slow run.

"Yeah. Not a five-mile hike though."

He grunted at her words, and she almost smiled.
The morning air chilled the dappled shade on the path.
Soon though, the running and the rising temperature
would warm her.

Squirrels rooted in the bushes, and birds called
back and forth to each other. She took a long breath.
Tanner had never run with her. Yeah, he hadn't done
anything much but take her to eat or to a movie and then
right back to her place—no, his place, as he'd reminded
her later, since he paid for it. Amazing that she thought
that was what it was all about. Life reduced to an hour or
two of food and entertainment and sex. Of course, a few
college classes and the idea that she would do something
with the rest of her life someday had also kept reality at
bay.

Tanner never talked about marriage or love, but
she'd figured that would come later. If she even wanted
that. Since her dad had walked out on them when she was
ten, she'd not been too impressed with marriage. If that
was all it was—something saying you were a couple with
some children, but you could still leave at any time—how
was it different from what she and Tanner had?

She had watched John Jergenson and Sharee
marry even after she tried to pull them apart, tried to
seduce him, but John had stayed faithful to Sharee, and
she'd wondered then if there was more to love and
marriage than she'd thought.

She sighed.

"Tired already?"

She cast a glance his way but continued running.
The sun broke through the trees here and there and
mottled the path as they jogged. Sweat moistened her
neck under her hair.

Jake grabbed her arm and pulled her to the right. "This shelter is empty. Let's take a break."

Water glimmered beyond it. China tugged her arm free, and they waded around the numerous tables to the railing. She looked past it into the dark water. The large pond was surrounded by bushes on every side. Nearby, a turtle ducked its head beneath the surface and swam away. Her gaze slid to Jake, but he stared across the pond to the other side.

In another moment, though, he turned and leaned back against the railing. "You do not have to tell me anything. Of course"—a smile titled his mouth upward—"I've been more than open with you."

She sent him a look from under her lowered brows and turned and also rested against the railing. She wasn't in a talking mood. What did he want, anyway? A full confession? She closed her eyes. No, he just wanted to know about the hair.

"It's up to me if I want to say anything."

"Yep."

She opened her eyes and frowned. "But you're pushing."

"I'm concerned about you. Is that wrong?"

She stared up at the shelter's ceiling, watching the breeze stir the cobwebs. "I guess you won't leave it alone."

He said nothing.

She let out an impatient breath. "All right. Ask what you want."

He faced her, and his arm brushed hers. "Why the wig?"

"I need it. I have no hair."

"Okay." He cleared his throat. "Why don't you have hair?"

China crossed her arms. "I had cancer."

He paused. "Had?"

"Yes."

"So the surgery…"

Her throat felt dry. She swallowed hard. One man had left already. What would this one do? Not that it mattered… She straightened. *No more running.*

"Yeah. I had a mastectomy. A *double* mastectomy." She didn't see his eyes drop to her chest, but she felt it. "They're fake."

"Uh…what?"

She forced the next words. "I have breast prosthesis. Fake boobs."

"Oh."

There. It was out. She forced herself not to cross her arms. She could almost hear his brain process the information.

He straightened and cleared his throat. "How…I mean…what a horrible thing to go through…at your age…at any age…I don't know…" His voice stopped.

He didn't know what to say. But what could he say, anyway? She didn't want platitudes. It was part of the reason—part—of why she'd told no one. Only her mother knew—and she'd sworn her mother to secrecy.

"But you're young. How…"

She forced a quick laugh. "That's what I wanted to know, too. I told the doctor his tests must be wrong. I made them do it again and send it to another lab." Her eyes grazed his, then ricocheted away. "The tests were the same."

The quiet held for a moment. "And you didn't come home?"

"No."

"Why? Your mom was here, your friends."

"And have everybody say I got what I deserved?"

His head bent until he caught her focus. "Is that what you thought they'd say?"

"It's what I deserved." And all she could think about. She'd failed as a woman in every way. The fear had paralyzed her for days. And after Tanner's betrayal, nothing mattered—or so she thought.

He grasped her arms and shook her gently. "Are you crazy? You didn't *deserve* this. No one deserves cancer."

Tears spilled over. Shame rose like heat in her face. She tried to turn away, but he shook her again— quick but with a tenderness she felt.

"You know all those people we pull out of the Gulf? With your kind of thinking, *most* of them deserve to be left there. Because most of them had heard the storm warnings or knew their boats needed work or forgot their flares—any number of dumb things. But do we leave them there? No, we risk our lives to get them. To pull them to safety."

The stupid tears wouldn't stop. She clasped her hands in front of her and bowed her head. Pain tore at her heart.

"And you know there's a spiritual element here, don't you?" His voice caressed her. "Christ does the same thing for us. I know what you said the other night, but Christ forgives. That was your testimony, wasn't it? That you'd found Him, and that He forgives—and heals."

His hands dropped from her shoulders, and the next thing she knew she was against his chest, soaking his shirt, and he was trying to caress her hair and laughing.

"How do you pat someone's hair when it's not their hair?"

She put her hand up. "Stop. Don't."

He slipped his hand around her back, holding her against him. "You know *thousands* of people have cancer every year. It's nothing to be ashamed of. In fact, be proud that you've beaten it."

Be proud? What a foreign thought...

Chapter 8

Jake groaned and grabbed the phone from his bedside table. Would he ever catch up on his sleep? The caller ID showed his copilot's name.

"What, dude? I'm almost asleep. What do you want?"

"You in bed already, J.T.? No hot date tonight?"

"It's eleven, and I'm trying to catch up on sleep. We're not going out, are we?"

"Nah. Lay back, guy. Take it easy. I just remembered something and needed to call."

"You just remembered, and it couldn't wait till morning?"

"Give me a break, will you? You know that woman from the news media that's been hounding us for an interview? She wanted to know when you'd be in next."

Great. Just what he needed. After this morning's emotional meeting with China and then tonight's meeting with the David's Mighty Men, he didn't need Lil the reporter prying into the ups and downs of his life at the Coast Guard.

"My schedule's the same as yours."

"Yeah, but she was asking specifically about you. Wanted to see if you could come in tomorrow for the interview. I think she likes you."

"Stuff it, man. I don't do lone-wolf stuff. What about Zeke? Don't they usually want to interview the rescue swimmer?"

"I guess she's highlighting the pilot. Step up, man. This is good promo for us. Her station is doing a

series on first responders, and we're in it. She said she
needs this soon. Besides, you can tell her about the teen
we rescued. That was a story."

Jake was quiet. Yeah, the teen was a story, but
they'd lost the mom. Not something he wanted to
concentrate on. "You gonna be there?"

"I'll back you up if you need it, teddy bear."

"You're getting on my nerves, Charley. You
know we both hate these things. You want to do eleven
AM with Lil and then get some lunch?"

"Sounds good to me. I'll even contact her for
you."

Jake growled. "The least you can do for calling
me so late."

Charley laughed, and Jake dropped the phone
back onto the bedside table.

Do a story on the boy. No. Not that the teenager
would want that anyway. Jake had not wanted to be
interviewed ever—not about his dad.

He punched his pillow, then balled it up under his
head. He'd told the teen it wasn't his fault, and it wasn't.
He'd wanted him to know that, to not have to live all the
years Jake had with the guilt. If he could see Mose's
guiltlessness, why couldn't he see his own?

He turned over and punched his pillow again. The
two situations were not identical.

No, but in Christ all is forgiven.

He threw the covers off, shoved his feet to the
floor, and stomped across the room. The boy's sobbing
had echoed the pain in his own heart. He missed his dad.
For fifteen years, he'd missed his dad.

He took a long breath. At some point, he needed
to get over this. Look at all that China had been through.
Her father just left. No reason, never to be seen again.
What would that have done to him? And yes, from what
she'd said, she'd probably acted out a number of years
because of it. But now, now she showed a developing

maturity that attracted him.

He stopped at the kitchen doorway. Attracted?

He stroked the stubble on his chin. She was definitely attractive. Yeah, so much that he kept looking away. But attracted to her?

She'd had a double mastectomy. *Think about that, J.T. You, Mr. Visual.*

He pulled a box of cereal from the shelf, grabbed a bowl and spoon, and got the milk from the refrigerator.

That hadn't done anything to stop the attraction, had it? Besides, couldn't they fix that nowadays?

China opened the door and gave Ryann what she knew was a lopsided grin.

Ryann's was simply there, full and wide. "I'm so glad you asked me over. I've wanted to see your place." Her eyes bounced past China and around the room. "Oooh, it's neat. I love it!"

"Not much, but it's mine for now."

"Let me see the bedroom and bath."

China laughed. "Sure. What there is of it."

"You're a great decorator. I love, love, love that fern print over the bed." Ryann scooted close to it. "It's an original. Did you do it?"

"No, not me, but I met a girl at one of the parks when I camped, and she did all sorts of artsy stuff. I just loved this one, so I bought it when I could."

"And you carried the theme into the bath. Lovely."

"You're good for the soul, you know it?"

Ryann came over and hugged her. "I am so glad you're back."

"Why? All I did was cause problems before." She led the way back to the living area. *This better play out okay, or Mr. Jake Osborne would hear from her.*

"Well, yeah, you did, but it was only because you

had your own problems. Oh! That didn't come out right. What I meant was you'd had a hard—"

"It's all right, Ryann. I understand. Have a seat. You want something to drink? Coffee, tea, water? I don't do sodas, but I have a lot of other stuff."

"No, I'm fine. Matt took me out for breakfast before I came over. So, what did you want to see me about?"

"It was really Jake's idea."

"Yeah?"

China hesitated. She had beefed up her courage before making the call this morning, and she could do it again. "I wanted to tell you a little more about what happened to me while I was away."

Ryann leaned forward. "You do?"

"Y…yes."

"Well, I'd love to hear it. You sounded like you had a rough time."

"I didn't think so at first. At first, I was completely blown away by Tanner, but he showed what a wolf he was when things got rough."

Ryann's face sobered. "I can relate."

The realization shot through her. Ryann really could relate to that part of her story. Ryann's boyfriend had disappeared when he found out Ryann was pregnant, and then she'd lost the baby.

China leaned forward and took her hand. "You know, I couldn't relate before. I didn't know how devastating that betrayal was. I'm sorry for what you went through."

Ryann pulled her lip in and said nothing, but then she smiled—a wavering smile, and China squeezed her hand.

"Guys are just jerks sometimes, aren't they?"

Ryann laughed. "Yeah, they are. But Matt's not. Matthew is the real thing."

China leaned back. "I'm glad to hear it. There's got to be a few good ones around."

"Like Jake."

"Jake?"

"Don't you think?"

"I'm just a problem to Jake. Someone else he has to watch out for. Anyway, he kind of pushed me to have you over and tell you the truth...about my surgery." She started to clamp her hand over her mouth. She didn't want Ryann to think she'd been forced to ask her over. And yet...well, she had. She'd never do this herself.

"Well, what's the truth?"

"The truth is..." She bit down on her lip and swallowed. The memory of hearing the diagnosis went through her, the unbelief, the shock. Her stomach clenched. She put her hand to the top of her head and pulled the wig off. "That I lost my hair."

Ryann's hand went to her mouth. "Oh, my goodness. It's a wig!"

Jake checked the rearview mirror again. The black van was two cars behind him, but there nevertheless. He returned his focus to the road. Hundreds of cars and trucks used this upcoming intersection—one of the busiest in the county. He needed to pay attention, not worry about some van in his rearview mirror. Whoever drove it must live near him and work near him. But a whisper of caution still feathered his insides.

He passed an oversized RV, a semi, and an SUV. In comparison, his Jeep seemed smaller than usual. But the traffic moved smoothly. Glad for that favor, he glanced at the clock and nodded. Almost eleven. Good. If the news reporter had arrived, maybe she and Charley would hit it off. That could take some questions and attention off him.

Jake pulled into the left-hand lane, preparing for

his turn. The light ahead turned red. He braked and glanced in the rearview mirror again. The black van swerved around the car right behind him and tried to ease into the space between them. The caution flickered to life. What was the driver doing? Did he see the red light?

The other car hit his brake, letting the van ease in. Jake could make out a round face, ball cap, and stringy hair. He tapped his brake hard, but the van appeared to speed up. It would hit him if he didn't do something. Jake glanced right. The lane was full. He jerked the wheel left, trying to make it to the median. The van slammed his rear bumper, and the Jeep spun out of control.

The airbag exploded in his face. Sound and pain mixed with the blare of horns and squeal of tires. A second later, the Jeep took another impact. The Wrangler rocked hard, and the side airbag detonated. Pain tore through his arm and shoulder. A third impact spun the Jeep in the opposite direction. Other horns sounded. Other crashes echoed through the fog surrounding him.

Then silence.

Jake moved his head, hoping to clear his ears, and coughed. White powder filled the air around him. The bag began to deflate, and he coughed again. Voices seemed far away, but a moment later a man stuck his head in his window, pushing at the airbag.

"Are you okay? Sit still. We've called an ambulance."

Jake's face burned. The airbag had sucker punched him. He turned his head slowly to see the speaker.

"Man, the other guy that ran into you took off."

The black van. The man with the ball cap and straggly hair. An image formed in Jake's mind. He reached for the seat belt.

"Wait here, guy. The ambulance is coming."

"Yeah." A lady and another man stood behind the first person. The lady's voice rose over the others'.

"Don't move. You got hit three times."

"I'm okay. I think." He struggled with the door. The other man pulled it open for him.

"I'd still not move, man. Your passenger side door is crushed. You're lucky they hit that side."

"Anyone else hurt?"

"Gotta be. Four cars were involved—and that's not counting that guy who caused it. He took off. But I got a partial plate. I'll give it to the police when they get here. They'll find him."

Sirens sounded in the distance.

Jake coughed again, and pain shot through his face and arms, his shoulders and neck. He leaned back against the Jeep's seat and decided to stay where he was.

"Hey! Let me through. That's a buddy of mine. Let me through." Charley's voice reached him. Then a hand landed on his arm and Charley's head was at his window. "Are you all right, J.T.? You okay?"

"I think. If the airbags hadn't beat me to a pulp, I'd be fine, anyway."

"You mean the ones that probably saved your life?"

Jake forced a grin. "Yeah. Those."

"Look, if you really didn't want to do this interview, why didn't you just say so?"

࿋

The police officer leaned forward. "So you're saying the man in the black van looked like the guy you saw at Juniper Springs?"

Jake let his legs swing below the edge of the hospital gurney. He'd waited awhile to get released. His injuries were superficial, thanks to the airbags. So the extra money he'd spent for the side airbags had paid off.

"Yes. The ball cap, the scraggly hair hanging out beneath it."

"And you think he's trying to kill you?"

"Yep. That's strong, I know. But someone shot at me—and this guy followed me from my apartment to where he ran into me. I don't know if he planned to do that or just took the opportunity there."

"Hmmm."

"Jake?" Pastor Alan put his head in the room.

"Yeah, I'm just answering some questions here."

"Okay. You all right? Daneen let me know you were here."

"The doctors are going to release me soon—at least, I hope it's soon."

China stepped past Alan. "I was at their place when Charley called."

"I'll get him for that. I told him I was fine."

"Yeah, well, he says you're pretty hardheaded, and since I know that's true, I came to drive you home. He's letting your captain—or whoever—know that you can't fly for a few days."

"Who told him to do that? I'll be able to fly tomorrow. No problem."

"Hardheaded, like he said."

Jake scowled at her and turned back to the police officer. "You know what? China saw this guy, too, and I bet she might have the same idea I have."

The officer lifted his brows but said nothing. Pastor Alan moved into the room and leaned against the wall, watching.

"The guy in the van that caused this accident had a ball cap and an unkempt head of hair hanging out from beneath it. Sound familiar to you?"

"Well, the ball cap and the hair sound like that man we saw where the alligator grabbed the dead guy."

"Yeah. That's what I was thinking."

"What make and color van was it?" the officer asked.

"The van? A black Dodge."

"Really?" China's voice rose a decibel. All three

men looked her way.

"What?" Jake asked.

"A man came to my house and tried to push his way in. Lucky for me, Sharee was there, and we forced him back out. But he pretended to be from the news station that Lil person belongs to. When I called, they said they have no reporter who looks like him on their payroll and no black Dodges."

The officer looked between them. "Did you report this?"

"No. I just thought it was someone who saw me on the news. You know, some weirdo."

Jake slid off the gurney. "But I think it's a wig."

China looked at him. He nodded. "I wouldn't have thought about it before, but now…well…a ball cap with straggly gray hair sticking out beneath. I mean, it's all we remember. What a way to hide how you look."

She frowned. "Are you trying to say this guy from Juniper Springs caused the accident?"

"And shot at me."

"Someone shot at you?" Her voice arced.

He waved a hand. "A few nights ago."

"So you think this guy is trying…trying to kill you?"

"Yeah, yeah. I do." His gaze settled on her. "And maybe you, too."

₰

Somehow they'd ended up at Panera's—as if food was a good idea when someone was trying to murder you. Jake took another bite of his sandwich and chased it with the coffee, rolling his neck to ease the tension and the tightness. His whole body ached.

China stayed fixated on her plate. He studied the mixed greens and nuts and strawberries and shook his head. How filling was that? When she raised her head, her deer-in-the-headlights look startled him.

His hand slid across the table, captured hers. "You okay?"

"Sure. I love being mixed up with some crazy who's trying to kill us."

"China—"

"It's not enough that I wind up with a loser who bails on me when I get cancer, that I have chemo and loose my hair, that…that I'll never be able to nurse a baby, but some wacko that we don't know is out there, and…" She stopped, closed her eyes.

His hand tightened on hers, and his mind raced. She'd kept those emotions hidden pretty well. "China?"

"Sorry. I just…"

The words sounded garbled. He tried to see her face. Was she crying? And… *Never nurse a baby?* He glanced around the room then back at her. Wow. What else had the cancer done to her? What else didn't he know?

He said her name for a third time.

She pulled her hand free and put her shoulders back. "I'm fine. Sorry. Just a moment's melt down."

"You don't always have to be fine. It's okay."

She shifted uncomfortably. "Yeah. My mother says that, too. That I don't have to be strong all the time, but—"

"No, you don't."

"But then who will? I can't just—"

Jake cut her off. "I will. Right now, let me do it. Just cry or rant on whatever you want to do." He got up, walked to her side of the table, pulled her up."

"What? What are you doing?"

"We're going for a ride. You can do whatever, say whatever—in the car."

"But our food…"

He glanced at the table. "Let's get a box. You can take me home. We'll eat there."

Her face skewed. "I…I…"

"You'll be safe. Don't worry."

She punched him. "I wasn't worried."

"Good." He grabbed her plate and his and nodded for her to get their drinks. "And while we're there, you can tell me about the chemo treatments and how you felt and all the other stuff you've never told anyone."

※

But, of course, she couldn't. At least, not everything. But his need to understand, his gentle questioning and concern—all of it was like a warm bath, scented, and healing to her soul. She'd tried to put it in the past, but the staggering pain of the whole situation had not disappeared simply because she wanted it to.

And Jake listened.

She smiled now, back in her own place thinking about it. He was an interesting person. Different. He'd also suggested calling Ryann at some time, talking with her.

Ryann…hmm…

Ryann's name had not made it into the news story about the alligator, but China decided to call her anyway. The girl needed to know what was going on.

China winced as Ryann's voice rose when she began to explain about someone running Jake off the road, about someone shooting at him, and that she and Ryann might be in danger, too. She gave a sigh when Ryann handed the phone to her dad.

"Mr. Byrd?"

"Yes. China, is it? What is Ryann trying to explain to me?"

He had taken the threat seriously but also said she and Jake could have made a wrong assumption. Maybe this had nothing to do with the alligator and the man's death.

True, and she needed to hear that; but still, when she put the phone down, she made sure all the doors were locked. Too bad she didn't have a dog or a gun. When the phone rang as she climbed into bed, she jumped.

"You doing okay?" Jake's voice warmed her.

The tightness in her shoulders eased. She leaned back against the pillows and smiled. "I'm okay, but thanks for checking on me."

"I need to call Ryann, too."

"I did a little while ago."

"Did you? How was she?"

"Flustered. But her dad took control."

"Yeah, he's a good man. Levelheaded. Her mom, too."

"But didn't she want to replace you with John in the youth group?"

"I can't blame people. Most of them have no idea what I've faced or how prevalent it is. But the important thing now is Ryann's safety—and yours."

"And yours."

"Yeah, but listen. I called the detective from Ocala that's in charge of this case. Guess what?"

"Just tell me."

"The man that was killed lives in the forest there, alone. They went out to his place, and guess what was growing on the acres of land he owns?"

"I don't know? Poppies?"

He snorted. "Not poppies. Marijuana."

"So he's growing his own?"

"Not just his. The detective said he's growing enough to ship out of state. They figured he could make five million dollars in state if they sold it to a cartel, and it would sell out of state for twice that amount."

"Aha. So, he did something he wasn't supposed to and our guy killed him."

"Yeah, the detective thinks so. But why meet at the Springs? Too many people."

"Actually, you know, when we got there—*early, by the way*—hardly anyone was there, and we passed no

one besides those girls. Hey, do you think *they're* all
right? Did they ever find them?"

"Yeah, local people. They weren't coming from
the spring, but from that side path. It goes to another
campground. They were going from that campground to
the swimming area. They don't even remember a man
behind them."

"Of course not. They were looking at you, Youth
Guy."

"China."

She laughed. "Okay. Well, I'm feeling better."

"Good. Did you check your locks like I asked?"

"Yes, yes. Whoever was here before put bolts on
the doors, so I'm okay."

"Well, take care of yourself, and keep an eye out
for anything strange. Call me—or the police—if you hear
anything. Got that?"

"Yes, Granny."

He grumbled something before saying good night.

She wouldn't tell him that she took some chairs to
sit in front of the doors and small breakables to sit in the
windowsills, nor that the warmth from his call lasted a
long time.

Chapter 9

As she left the tattoo parlor, China rolled her shoulders back and beamed at the sky. The tattoo artist had understood exactly what she wanted, and his design achieved more than she expected. An intricate design with words around it.

She stood a moment, arms around herself, smiling. She couldn't wait to show Jake. What would he say?

"China?"

The woman's voice startled her. She swung around and almost collided with the "lady in red." A strange way to address anyone, but China couldn't remember her name—just the clothes she'd worn at the meeting at church. Today, a red scarf draped around her neck and highlighted an all-black pants outfit. "What? Oh…uh, Mrs.…hello." Heat flooded China's face as she stumbled over the name.

The woman glanced at the tattoo shop and back at China. "So you're getting *another* tattoo?"

"Uh, yes."

Her gaze traveled up and down China's form. "You don't think that one tattoo you have is enough? Of course, you may have others that no one can see—well, no one at church, anyway."

China's throat tightened. The woman's antagonism hit her, and she swallowed.

"I'm not sure why you came back to church, China, but hopefully you've changed. But if I were you, I'd stay away from tattoo parlors. Especially since the tattoo you have tells everyone what you are…were."

"I'm not sure what you mean."

"You can't hide it, you know. My husband knows—well, not him, of course. Another man told him."

"Told him what?"

The woman leaned closer. "He knows you were a porn star."

China jerked back. "That's not true."

"You can't deny it. His...his friend remembered the tattoo. Very hard to miss, the man said."

"I...I..."

The lady tossed her red scarf over her shoulder. "Don't worry. I won't tell anyone, but heavens! First the pastor, then the youth pastor—and now you. What is our church coming to? There's talk as it is, but if they knew this...well... You can see the talk, can't you? The *reformed* youth pastor picks a porn star to help with the youth." Her eyes rounded. She gave an exaggerated shrug, walked past China, and disappeared around the corner.

China stared after the woman. The air around China seemed short of oxygen. It grayed her vision until all she could see was the place where the lady in red had disappeared.

※

China placed the suitcase in the middle of the living area and looked around. Her heart thudded. She loved the house, the pictures, the colors, but it didn't matter. How could she go back to church knowing...knowing some of the men had seen...whatever was on the internet? It would be too humiliating.

God, I thought you brought me back here for a reason, but I can't do this. What if Jake hears this? What if they fire him? And Pastor Alan? Pain stabbed through her, but she couldn't think about that, couldn't think either about how much Jake had come to mean to her.

Tears started again. She brushed her palms over her face. Stupid. What good did it do to cry?

Her other suitcase sat in the bedroom, with clothes scattered across the bed. Her tent was in the garage. She'd find a campsite tonight and then decide where to go from there, what to do about college, about paying the rent here. Hopefully, she wouldn't have to ruin her credit.

She went to the window and looked up and down the street. No one, no cars. Good. Whoever had followed her from the tattoo shop wasn't there. At least, she thought someone had followed her. Not that she had noticed at first, but after a few miles, she finally realized the white Camry always stayed a car or two behind her.

Her focus went to the front window again. She could have made a mistake. After all, why would a white Camry follow her anywhere? Then the car had turned off a few blocks before she got home. To be safe, she'd called Ryann and let her know and told her to call Jake later. Not now, China had said. She needed some time to herself.

She went to pack her other suitcase and stood and stared at the clothes, the heaviness inside freezing her.

Pounding on her door jarred her. She glanced around at the bed and at her suitcase. If Ryann had come over, what would she tell her?

The knocking started again, then Jake's voice. "China, are you in there?"

Her heart skipped. What was he doing here? She closed the bedroom door and went to the living area.

"China!"

"I'm coming. Keep your clothes on." Oh yeah. That was the thing to say. She hesitated a moment, then threw the door open. "Are you supposed to be up and driving?"

He stepped through the doorway and glanced around. "I'm not here about me. Ryann said someone was following you."

Cheez! She'd told the girl not to say anything yet.

"I'm fine. A false alarm."

"You didn't answer your phone." He tilted his head. "And you've been crying."

She turned her head away. How had she missed his call?

"What's up? And what's this?"

She glanced his way. The suitcase rested on the floor next to him.

"Are you going someplace?" He stepped closer. "Are you that scared?"

"Yes. No, I mean. I'm fine. I just need to get away for a while."

"Why? Because you can't go somewhere alone. Not when you may have…someone out to hurt you."

"Or wanting to kill us?" His closeness bathed her in warmth. She stepped back, putting her hands up, fending off the pull of his presence. "I'm fine. I told you. That has nothing to do with this. I just need to get away."

"Why?"

"Why?"

"Yes, what else is going on that you need to get away?"

"Nothing you should worry about."

He stepped back into her space again. "I do worry about you. Why are you crying?"

How could she tell him? And she didn't want to lie. The feeling of being trapped was new. "It's nothing. You need to leave. I'm fine."

"China." His hand touched her arm. "Is this about your hair, your mastectomy?"

"No, I—"

"Did someone find out? Did they say something?"

"My hair is the least of my worries right now."

"Then what is it? Something's up."

"Nothing's up. Will you just—"

"I can't believe Ryann would cause this. If it's something she said, and I encouraged you to tell her then—"

"Ryann did nothing."

"What did she say?"

Her throat tightened. Would he ever give up? "Just drop it, will you? I'm fine. If I want to get away, that's my business. I don't answer to you or anyone else."

His brow wrinkled. "I'm not saying you do. But—"

Arguing was too hard, especially when she wanted to be in his arms more than anything, to have him hold her and tell her everything would be okay. But it wouldn't be. She stepped away from him and headed to her bedroom. "I'm not keeping this up. Let yourself out."

When she threw open the door, he was right behind her. "At least tell me where you're going."

"Nowhere you need worry about." She turned to thrust him out, but he'd stopped at the doorway. His eyes rested on what was past her, on the bed. She followed his glance. Quiet settled over the room.

"So, how long are you planning on being gone?"

"I…don't know."

"But definitely not just overnight." His face stilled. "Your friend call?"

"What?"

"Tanner. Does he want to see you again?"

Her mouth opened, but nothing came out for a moment. "How…how dare you! You think I'd run to him if he called?"

"I'm not sure what to think." His mouth moved, twisted. "Something is going on though. And you're right. You don't have anyone to answer to—especially me." His focus went to the bed again. "But you're certainly going somewhere. Running off—without a good-bye—to anyone."

The tone of his words caught her attention. He

sounded upset, but how could he think she'd go back to Tanner?

Her jaw tightened. "I would never go back to Tanner."

"Then the question is, who are you running to or from?"

"Neither. You've got this confused."

"Do I? Want to tell me how?"

She bit her lip and said nothing.

His blue eyes darkened. He watched her a moment longer, then nodded and headed for the door.

"Jake, wait."

He pulled the door open and threw a scowl in her direction. "Why? You've got this all planned out it seems. Sorry if I messed anything up. But at least call the police and tell them where you're going."

"No, I—" She stepped forward and grabbed his arm. "Will you stop? What's wrong with you?"

"I don't like being lied to."

"I haven't lied to you."

"You haven't told me the truth either."

She closed her eyes and swallowed. Her throat tightened. "I…I don't know what you're thinking, but you're wrong about it."

"What am I wrong about?"

"I'm not running to anyone."

"Then you're running away."

"No, I…" She swallowed. He said nothing. "I can't. I—"

"Can't what?"

Her throat hurt. She pushed down the pain. "It's too hard."

He stared at her for a moment, and then he shut the door quietly. "What is?"

"I…the lady in red."

"The lady in red? What are you talking about?"

"The other night. At church. She was so rude to

you."

"You mean Mrs. Swinson? During the vote?"
She nodded.

"Yeah, well, she's…one of a kind, all right. But what has that to do with you leaving?"

She moved to the middle of the room and stared at the floor. "Mrs. Swinson told me the church would be better off without me."

"*She what?*"

"Well, not exactly, but she inferred that."

He closed the space between them. "How did that ever come up? And that's a bunch of junk. Why would you listen to something like that?"

"She's probably right."

"No, she's not. What else did she say?"

China shook her head. "Nothing. Why?"

"Because there's got to be more. What else did she say to make you run away?"

She turned toward the window. She was running. Again.

"I'm not leaving until I hear the whole thing."

Her throat closed. She didn't know if she could say the words.

Jake stepped up close behind her, his breath warm on her neck. "Tell me."

"She…she said a friend of her husband's saw me." China put her hand to her throat. "He saw me on a porn site."

"He saw you on a porn site?" His voiced jumped a decimal. "Is…have you…"

She shook her head. "No. I mean, not that I know of. But I started thinking. What if Tanner took pictures and put them on the internet?"

"Did he take pictures?"

"He wanted to. He talked about it. I said no, but…well, I always wondered about those little hidden cameras."

Jake's jaw tightened. "This man makes me angrier every time I hear about him."

"He recognized the tattoo."

"Who? Mr. Swinson?" Jake turned her to face him. "That's how he knew it was you?"

She nodded but kept her head down.

"That's all he saw then—a body and a tattoo. I doubt it was you. It was Twila James. I'm not letting you leave for something like this."

"What if it was me?"

"It wasn't."

Tears pooled and slid down her cheeks. She covered her face with her hands. "How could I live with that? Knowing that they…"

Jake drew her to him. She rocked from side to side and tried to hold back the sobs.

"Hey, stop. Don't do this." He caressed her back. "That man did not see you. He saw a tattoo like yours."

"And a body."

"Well, your body is clothed—most of the time."

"*Most of the time?*"

"I mean mostly clothed. You have some pretty short shorts."

"I haven't worn those since…" She stopped. She hadn't worn them since she knew what a problem they were for him.

"You're not letting the devil get the best of you. You ran out of state a few years ago, and look where it got you."

"Do you think she'll tell anyone?"

"Well, then she'll have to explain how her husband knows about this."

"She said he has a friend who told him."

"Yeah, and we all believe that. His friend just happened to mention that he watches porn, and then he describes the tattoo the porn star had. Sounds like a regular conversation, doesn't it? Not. Not unless one porn junkie is talking to another."

She laid her head against his chest. She felt safe here, against him. Why couldn't things be like this? Why did they have to be so hard? *I'm trying to do right, Lord, and I keep getting slammed.*

"Don't go anywhere." Jake's words sounded rough. "Where would I find another person who's as much help with the youth? As much fun? Besides, you promised to go boating with me."

"I didn't promise."

"Oh yes, you did. Anyway, you're stronger than this. You need to remember you're forgiven. You're free in Christ. Don't let anyone take that from you."

She lifted her head and searched his eyes. His head tilted, and his gaze fell to her mouth. A moment later, his eyes rose, questioning, but the pause was short. He bent his head, his mouth finding hers, covering hers. She leaned into him, absorbing the feel and taste of him. His arms tightened, and he deepened the kiss.

When he finally drew back, his voice came rough and uneven. "Don't go anywhere."

Chapter 10

Jake tied up his Bryant 233 bowrider to the dock and stood looking at the parking lot. The morning air held a touch of chill still. In another two weeks that would pass. Summer bumped spring out of the way early in Florida. Still, a morning ride on the water, sun rising, never ceased to unwind him.

But he couldn't quite keep his mind off yesterday and the day before, comparing the China he knew with the person Mrs. Swinson thought she knew. When he'd fought free of the addiction three years ago, he'd come to understand that many women "acting" on the porn sites were trafficked, held as slaves even, forced to pretend they liked what they were doing. Something had moved in his heart two days ago as China shook against his chest. It slid like a steel door into place. Even if the women weren't trafficked—even if they were porn "stars"—never again would he be part of degrading them—through the voyeurism of the internet or any other way.

He inhaled and thought about the other thing. They'd taken a step forward in their relationship, which he hadn't anticipated. All he'd thought about last night was that the girl must have him under some kind of spell.

He smiled, stretched, and thought about stepping back onto the boat again to get his coffee, but just then she drove into the lot. She parked beside Charley's car and the trailer. Charley had lent it to Jake since his Jeep was still in the shop. Two other cars with trailers had parked nearby, but no one else was around.

China walked toward him. He hadn't worried

about her wearing a bikini. That wouldn't happen, but he had wondered about what she'd wear on the boat and to swim in.

Yeah, they'd talked about swimming. He watched her smile echo his as she stepped onto the dock. A longish pair of shorts and a bright sleeveless tee over what could be a one-piece suit. Wide straps at the edge of the T-shirt. He'd find out later. Somehow the idea of the tattoo didn't worry him as much as he thought it would. He'd determined night before last that it would not define their relationship. Big word. Relationship.

Once she regained her footing the other day, she'd determined to go back to church, head high. Then she'd agreed to go boating today and agreed to a swimming lesson—with or without the wig.

He grinned as he caught her hand and helped her onto the boat. She'd gone from running away to pushing her limits.

"Good morning."

The boat rocked, and she grabbed his arm. "Yeah, good morning—I think. Not sure why I agreed to this."

His chuckle had her sending him a look between narrowed eyes.

"Because you can't resist a challenge."

"Hmm. Maybe that's why I'm going back to church, but this—"

"I'll get you a life jacket in a minute. You'll feel better."

"She'll feel better once you get this boat started and get out of here." A man's voice jumped between them.

Jake spun around. The man stood on the dock. His dark hair, stocky build, and ball cap pulled low looked menacing enough without the hand in his jacket pocket that pointed at them.

"I have a gun. Don't give me any problems, or I will use it. Back up to the other side. Both of you."

China's head jerked Jake's way, eyes wide. He caught her arm and pulled her back. If the man wanted money or the boat…

The man stepped down into the boat and clutched the back of one seat as the boat rocked. The hand on the gun never wavered. He spread his feet and balanced himself.

Jake dropped China's arm and leaned forward. If the man lost his balance—

"Don't try anything." He pulled the gun from his pocket and aimed it at China. "If you try anything, she gets shot. You understand?"

Jake nodded. The man looked familiar. "What are you doing? What do you want?"

"You don't know? Then maybe all of this is for nothing."

"You're the man from Juniper Springs." China's voice shook. "You killed that other man."

"The girl earns a star. I thought the US Coast Guard here would have it first."

Recognition hit. No scraggly hair, but the nose and mouth were the same. If so, he'd tried to kill Jake before, had tried to break in to China's home. Jake glanced toward the parking lot. If another boater pulled in…

The man waved the gun at Jake and toward the wheel. "Start this thing and get going."

Jake hesitated. Wouldn't they be safer here? The gun moved. Its barrel pointed at China. The hair on the back of Jake's neck rose.

"I said get going. Move!"

Jake stepped to the wheel. The guy wasn't comfortable on the boat. That could be a plus, but what was he planning? China hadn't moved. Was she frozen in fear or planning something herself? *Lord, don't let her do anything that will get her killed.*

"We'll have to untie."

The man moved toward the stern and nodded to China. "Do it, and remember I have the gun on you." He shot a look at Jake. "Don't try anything."

Jake met China's shocked stare. "Untie the boat and then push the boat away from the dock." If he could somehow leave her on the dock, it would only be Jake and the other man.

"Don't get any ideas. Untie the boat, then get back in here and push off. I can shoot you on the dock as well as here."

"If you're planning on shooting us, we might as well stay right here." Could he jump the man while his attention was on China?

"All right. I'll shoot the girl first."

"No!" The word burst from Jake. "No. What's the problem anyway? Why are you doing this?"

The man ignored him. "Untie the boat. Now."

China worked with the rope, then threw it back into the boat.

"Jump in, sweetheart. We're waiting for you."

She glanced at Jake, then crawled unsteadily over the side.

"Okay. Push off." When China just stood there, he swung the gun between her and Jake. His voice rose. "I said push off."

"She's never been on a boat before. She's not sure what to do."

"Push away from the dock." The words were almost a shout.

China leaned over and pushed against the dock. The boat drifted out a foot or two.

"Okay, Mr. C.G. Take off."

Jake eased the throttle upward.

"Out to the Gulf."

Jake heard some scuffling and jerked his head around in time to see the man shove China forward. She grabbed Jake's arm. Her gaze caught his, the uncertainty and fear clear. The man could kill them both.

"Stand next to the boyfriend. I need you both in view."

"What do you want?" Jake threw the words over his shoulder.

"You bragged about how you would recognize me again. Remember that? You pulled Davy from the alligator's mouth and then said how you could identify me."

Jake remembered. He'd looked at the man hard when he went by them that day because he'd wondered about the girls' safety.

"He's the man that came to my house," China said under her breath.

"I work at WJPY. I'm one of Lil's camerapersons. She wanted to highlight the Coast Guard here on that program of hers. I couldn't take the chance you'd recognize me."

Jake grunted. "So you tried to kill me that night?"

"Let's say I wanted you out of the way."

Jake could sense the man's closeness. Could he knock the gun from his hand before he got a shot off? But what if he hit China?

The boat bounced, hit another wave, and bounced again.

The man's hand grabbed his arm. "Slow down."

Jake's muscles bunched, but China was too close. He shot a look over his shoulder. The man definitely wasn't comfortable on the boat. Jake could say most anything, and the guy might believe it.

"If we go too slow, the boat will rock and get swamped. You wanted out in the Gulf. Well, there are waves out here." He ducked his head toward China. "Sit down."

Her head bent in his direction. Had she heard him? A moment later, she slowly lowered herself onto the seat.

She threw a look behind her. "Why did you kill that man?"

"He wanted to pull out. I needed the money."

"You were selling the pot they found?"

"Yeah."

Jake monitored the conversation, waiting. China was still in the line of fire, but if he could hit the right wave, he might throw the man off balance long enough to get the gun. He focused on the water. The blue stretched to the horizon. Bright sunshine and clouds added a surreal feeling to what was happening. They passed a small island on their right, then another. Two more rose from the Gulf of Mexico a little farther out.

"See that far island? Head there."

Jake grunted again.

They hadn't passed another boat, but the possibility they would was good. Would it help though? He didn't like the sound of the island. Would the man just drop them off? To be rescued soon thereafter? He doubted it.

"If something happens to us, they'll suspect you. You've done too much already."

Jake watched a wave form, bigger than the others. *Wait for it. Wait...* He turned the boat and hit it straight on. The boat slammed against it, white spray shooting up on either side, then slammed down again. He started to turn, but the man jabbed the gun against his back.

"You did that on purpose. If you're dead, I can still drive this thing."

"They'll catch you."

The guy took a step back. "They don't know who they're looking for. If you hadn't brought Davy up, if he'd disappeared as I planned, I'd have kept the business going, and no one would ever know."

"Someone would have found him. You couldn't be sure an alligator would get him. That was a fluke."

"I hadn't planned on killing him. He was my best

friend. It got out of control."

"Your best friend? Right."

The gun jabbed his back again. "We grew up together. Hung out at Juniper Springs on weekends. Picked up girls." The man's voice fell. "We met to talk. He grows the stuff near here. I live in the city and sell it. He wanted to quit."

"And you didn't."

"I told you. I needed the money. He was going to quit anyway."

"So you shot him."

"We argued. I didn't think."

The boat was eating up the distance to the island. He had to make a decision. "But you're planning this." Planning to kill them. The man would kill them both to sell weed. Kindling caught fire in his gut, eating up the hesitation and fear.

"I had to. When Lil started talking about the interview with you, I knew I had to do something."

"You were in the black van?"

"Yes."

The flame inside jumped and grew. The island was close, the sand beneath the boat shelving already. He needed to do something. *Now*. He threw the helm over hard and pulled the throttle to neutral. The boat bucked and slid around, water spraying into the air. China's sharp gasp and the man's curse sounded together. Jake spun around. The man lurched across the seat and fell to the floor. The gun flew from his hand.

Jake landed on top of him and shoved his arm under the man's chin. "Get the gun. China! Get the gun!"

The man heaved and twisted, but Jake pushed into his throat until he began to choke.

China scooted past him and picked up the gun. "I've got it."

"Back away from us and keep the gun trained on him."

"Okay."

The man tried to push Jake's arm away, but Jake put his face close his. "You want to breathe again? Then stop fighting."

The man stilled. Jake waited for a moment, then eased back. "China, if he—"

Something slammed against his head. He reared back. The man sent another fist to Jake's jaw, then shoved upward. Jake fell back but grabbed the man's foot as he reached for a seat. A moment later, the foot smashed into Jake's face. Light pulsed in and out in front of him.

The sound of a scuffle followed, and a line of curses. "Give me the gun."

China's "No!" rang loud and clear.

Jake hauled himself up against the side of the boat. China screamed, and the sound of a splash followed. He jerked around. The man was leaning over the stern, and China had disappeared.

He lunged to the first seat and yanked it up. An old sleeping bag enclosed in plastic lay on top. He snatched it out and threw it over the side, then grabbed one of the life vests beneath it.

"Jake!" Splashing and China's panicked voice came from the other side.

The guy turned, eyes wide, and charged. Jake tried to sidestep, but the man caught the vest and shoved it into Jake's face.

"He...lp!" China's garbled yell rose again.

Jake leaned down, grasped the man about the waist, and pushed him backward into the other seat.

"Oof!"

He snatched up the life vest and leapt to the side. "China! Grab this!"

Something hit him from behind. He flew forward, tried to catch the side of the boat, couldn't find a hold, and plunged over the side. He surfaced, spitting, the boat just feet away. When he spun around, he didn't see China, only the life preserver. Fear rocketed through him. He whipped around once more. She surfaced near him, coughing, slapping the water.

He caught the vest and shoved it at her. "Grab it!"

Coughing, choking, she groped for it and caught hold. Her eyes were wide, mouth gasping for breath.

"You'll be all right. Hold on to it." He couldn't get close in case she panicked and tried to crawl on top of him.

Behind him, the boat started. He twisted around. The boat moved forward. It gathered speed then did a slow turn.

Jake felt his heart drop. The man was coming back. Was he planning to run over them? Shoot them? He jerked his head in China's direction.

"Find the straps, and put your arms through them."

Her look was dazed.

"Do it now. You hear me?"

She nodded and tried to maneuver the vest.

The boat engine grew louder. He swam over and pulled the straps over her shoulders. "Just keep this clutched in front of you. Swim to the island." He turned her around and gave her a shove.

"What?"

"He's coming back. Swim to the island. Kick your feet. Hold the vest. Kick your feet. Go!"

He turned and swam away from her. The guy couldn't hit them both at once. Hopefully, he'd think Jake more important to run over.

The sound of the engine grew. Jake twirled in the water, watched for another second or two, took a deep breath, and dove. Blue water filled his vision. The sand met him. It was shallow. Fifteen feet at most. Was it deep enough to defray a bullet? The white bottom of the boat, a thousand bubbles in its wake, went by.

He surged upward.

When he broke water, he gasped for breath. The bowrider's engine still throbbed. He twirled. The boat hadn't stopped, but was circling. How many times could he do this?

I need some help, Lord.

He waited until the boat came close again. The man stayed at the wheel. Jake took a deep breath and dove. Just before the water closed over his head, he saw something black against the white sand. *The gun.* He dove toward it. His hand closed over it. He looked up and saw the swirl of the boat passing again. Shoving off the bottom, he shot to the surface. The air felt raw in his airway.

Jake glanced back toward the island. China was closer to him than he'd thought. His heart jumped. Why hadn't she headed for the island?

She waved her hand at him and pointed. The boat had made its turn and headed back. He treaded water, lifting himself a little higher, making sure the man came his way and not China's. The boat bore down on him, its speed lifting the hull from the water.

He didn't have a clean shot. It was almost on him before he moved. He swam hard, plowing the water with his hands. Then he turned, did his best to aim, and fired. The man's head came around. Jake shot again and again. The portside of the boat lifted as it swerved away. Behind it, in the distance, he saw another boat.

Yes!

China yelled something, but he kept his eye on the bowrider as it headed in the other direction. Was the man gone for sure? The boat slowly disappeared back toward land. The other boat seemed to grow as it came in their direction. It took a moment before he realized that the course it was on would not bring it close to the island but would take it farther south.

Jake swung his arms and hollered. Behind him,

China's voice rose, too. But the boat never corrected course. He watched it disappear against the turquoise sky.

She'd been shivering for a while, no matter how tight he held her, how he wrapped his arms and legs around her. They'd made it to the island, and the sleeping bag had floated ashore an hour or so later. Still in the plastic bag he'd sealed it in. The small island had some brush and five palm trees. Not much shade. So the bag, strung between two palms, had protected them from the sun's rays all day, but no water and no food had left them weak and parched

No boats all day either. They weren't that far from the mainland, and he'd thought for sure a boat would come within shouting distance, but none had. Maybe tonight. A romantic night on the water for someone could end in his and China's rescue.

Rescue. He stared up at the night sky. He'd left a float plan, as always, with Charley, and Charley's car was still sitting in the parking lot with Jake's trailer hitched to it. Charley would know they should have returned before dark. He would have called in the alarm by now. They'd probably hear the helo tonight, but they had no way to signal them. Tomorrow then.

The dark night highlighted the stars' brightness. Yes, a romantic place—if they weren't stranded, if the constant wind hadn't penetrated to their bones. The sleeping bag's coziness, its warmth, the pleasure of having China tucked in next to him, had evaporated as the night wore on. Since the temperature had dropped, all he thought about was keeping her warm.

"They'll find us. It's what they do."

Her back was to him, and her slight nod was not an affirmation of belief as much as a way to indicate she'd heard him. Besides fighting the shock of nearly drowning, she was now stranded without food or water.

And the loss of her wig had bothered her all afternoon. It bothered him at first, too, but as the day wore on, he'd become used to the pixieish hair.

"O death, where is your sting? Or grave, where is your victory?"

Her trembling stopped. "What?"

"It just came to mind. If we die here, we haven't done anything but graduate to a higher plane, a higher life, being with God."

Her silence lasted a few minutes. Did he sound like they wouldn't make it? Like he'd given up? "Look, that just came to mind. In no way am I saying—"

"To be absent from the body is to be present with the Lord. That's what you're saying."

"I…yes, but I didn't mean—"

She broke across him again. "I know what you mean. In all this, I've wondered where God is, and yet He's still here. He hasn't left."

"No, He hasn't. China?"

She lifted her head a little. "Yes?"

"Do you think you'll let people know at church about your…about the cancer now?"

"You think I should?"

"It's up to you. Of course, when we get rescued, and we get back to the mainland, the media will be there. They'll probably take pictures."

She sucked in her breath. "My hair."

"Yeah. It's fine, you know. My grandmother just ties a scarf around her head and runs out."

"Well, I'm not your grandmother."

He chuckled. "That I know, but it's okay to be who you are."

She started to laugh.

He drew back an inch or two and wished he could see her face. "What? That was funny?"

"*You* are funny. I am okay—or more okay with who I am. You know when that started?"

"No."

"That day you opened my door and saw me taking off my wig. I wanted to shoot you, and yet it was the best thing for me. I didn't have to hide anymore. It was okay to be me."

"I certainly didn't get that picture."

"No, I guess not."

"You threw me out."

"Of course." She tried to turn in the sleeping bag, but stopped and shivered as the wind gust increased. "I cried for a long time."

His arms tightened. "I'm sorry."

She said nothing for a moment. "No. I needed it. I hadn't cried since Tanner ditched me. I told myself I wouldn't, but I needed to. Cried for my foolishness, his coldness, my…my body."

"Your breasts." It popped out. He hadn't meant to say it, even though he'd thought it. She had to grieve the loss—like the loss of a limb.

She stilled. "Yes."

"Can you, you know…" *How do I ask this, Lord?*

"I couldn't have them…reconstructed…right then because of the chemo. Now I…I just need to do it."

"You know I'd love you even without them." He stopped. Where had that come from? Now she wasn't only still, but stiff. Was it the truth? Was he in love with her?

She twisted in the bag until she faced him. "What are you saying?"

"I'm not sure. I mean, I'm sure about the 'without' part."

"The 'without' part?"

"Look. That came out wrong."

"So, you don't love me?"

"No. I mean, yes. No, what I mean is I hadn't meant to say that."

"Obviously not." She started to turn away again,

but he caught her and held on. She squirmed.

"Stop. Listen a minute. I don't know where all this is going, but what I said is true. I care for you. It could be love, but I haven't thought it through yet. I just wanted you to know it's not…not dependent on your breasts." They were both silent. What now? "Of course, if you had them rebuilt, reconstructed, whatever, that would be a plus." His voice faltered. What was he saying?

"You…you would accept me as I am?"

Jake could barely hear her voice. He had thought about this a long time last night. Her breasts or lack of them didn't affect the way he felt about her, didn't stifle the admiration he had for what she'd been through and what she'd pulled herself out of. And he was attracted to her. No doubt about that. No doubt what he was feeling now.

"Do you know what you're saying?"

Her breath warmed his neck. He tightened his hold. "Of course." He moved his head to find hers and found the top of her head. He kissed her hair. She stiffened again.

"Look up here."

She snuggled in closer to his neck and shook her head.

"No? You asked if I knew what I was saying. I do. Lift your head up." He dropped his mouth to her forehead, then the top of her nose. "China." Her head moved, and his mouth found the top of her lip, then shifted lower. Her lips parted, and he was kissing her with a passion that surprised him. Her body pushed into his, and he groaned.

They'd solved the cold problem.

His mouth slid off hers and slipped to her ear. She jerked against him and trembled. "China." His voice sounded husky, even to his own ears. *Slow down, J.T.* He drew his head back, cleared his throat. "We'd better stop this."

Her mouth was against his neck, soft kisses tracing along his collarbone.

His breath jumped again. "China."

"You're going to wear out my name."

"There's only so much room in this sleeping bag, and I'm trying to keep us from going somewhere we might regret."

She stopped and pulled her head up. Relief washed through him.

"Did you mean what you said?" Her voice wavered.

"Yes, I did. The fact that I don't want to take advantage of our situation does not mean I didn't. You know, there was a time when not taking advantage of a woman was a good thing."

"I know, but you started this."

"I did." He forced a chuckle. "I just didn't realize how hot you thought I was."

"You…you egotistical…male!" She pushed against him and pummeled his chest. He laughed and tugged her closer until she stopped.

"At least you're warm now." He chuckled again, and she fought against his hold. "No, no, don't go anywhere. Not that you can." When she settled against him, he let his chin rest on her head, on the short, soft hair.

She stirred. "What were you doing with a sleeping bag in your boat anyway?"

"I always carry it in case I want to sleep under the stars. Find an island like this one and camp for the night."

"You're kidding. By yourself?"

"Yes, by myself. But I'm hoping not always by myself. This is more fun."

"Fun. Yeah."

"Could be, if we weren't stranded."

"Trying to convince me?"

"I think so. Yes."

She didn't answer.

"China."

"There you go again. I'm right here."

"What are you thinking?"

"That they'll find us. That's what they do."

"You're right. They will."

"Lord."

Her voice in prayer surprised him.

"Thank you for Jake, for saving us and using Jake, for his integrity, for your salvation, and thank you for getting us out of this place. Help the people looking for us to find us and keep us safe until they do. In Jesus' name. Amen."

The lump in his throat was as much a surprise as her prayer. "Thank you for Jake," she'd said. "For his integrity," she'd said. He turned his head to search the sky. The scattered stars blinked between the branches of dark palms, and Jake sent his own heartfelt thank-you up to the God of heaven.

≥

The whump-whump of the helicopter's propeller shook him awake. His eyes snapped open, and soft morning light hit them. He reached across China and yanked down the zipper of the sleeping bag.

"China, move. Get up. They're here." He crawled over her. She moved groggily.

He glanced around for something to wave. Nothing bright or reflective. He ran for the water. The sound of the helo's prop grew stronger. He glanced skyward. It looked close. Surely someone would see them. Someone had to be looking this way. What did they have to wave?

He jumped up and down, waving his arms. "Hey!"

Their flight pattern didn't bring them as close as he wanted. Had anyone seen him? No indication they had.

"Here. Use this. Use this." China was dragging the sleeping bag.

"It's blue. They'll never see it. But get out here. Your neon shirt might help." She ran up next to him, jumped up and down, and waved her arms. "Don't leave. Don't leave. You have to see us!"

His heart galloped like a racehorse. *Is this how every survivor felt? This desperation?* He swung his arms and shouted.

"Here. Take this!" She thrust her shirt into his hand. The top of the one-piece swimsuit she wore fit like a sleeveless T-shirt. "Go. Get in the water. Wave it."

He tore out into the water, swimming hard, then held the shirt over his head and shook it back and forth. "Somebody look back this way. Look back." But his heart dropped as the helo angled away and slowly disappeared. He treaded water for a while longer, hoping to see it reappear, but the sound of the prop was a bare echo now.

The water surprised him with its chill as he swam back to where he could stand. He waded to shore. China still held the sleeping bag. She was weaving slightly, her head bowed.

"I'm sorry. They didn't see it. And it was one of ours."

"Did you ever think how many times you passed over someone and didn't see them?"

"Hey. They'll be back. If this is their flight pattern, they'll come by again."

"But what if it isn't? What if they just decided to take a peek this way?"

"Think on good things." He handed her shirt to her. "Here. Thanks."

"No, keep it. Give me yours. That way I won't have to take it off again."

"I don't think yours will fit me."

"Just keep it by you, Mr. Coast Guard."

He pulled his shirt off and handed it to her. She tugged it over her head. The gray T-shirt hung on her. The Coast Guard logo—Honor, Respect, Devotion to Duty—stood out in orange letters. She opened her arms and spun around. "What do you think?"

"I think I was right."

"You're right? About what?"

He reached for her and pulled her into his arms. "That I love you. And if we ever get rescued, I plan on proving it to you."

She stopped moving and searched his eyes with hers. "You could do that now."

"Oh?" He gave her a slow smile and then lowered his head to hers.

It took a minute this time for the whump-whump of the blades to penetrate his thoughts.

He yanked free and began waving her shirt. "Hey! Hey!"

China jumped up and down beside him. The orange-and-white chopper came to a hover above them, the wind from its blades whipping their bodies. Jake slipped his arm around China, drawing her close to protect her from the wind and sand.

Shielding his eyes with the back of his hand, he looked up and watched the door open. A person stood there for a moment, then grabbed the hoist. Jake watched the familiar figure being lowered to the ground.

Rescue. What a beautiful word.

A minute later, Zeke stood before them, eyes dancing. "Wes told us he saw you, but we made him beg us to turn around."

China pulled her head from the protection of Jake's chest. "Praise God he did! Who's Wes?"

"The flight mechanic." Jake pointed at the chopper and the man leaning out the door. "The hoist guy. The medic. The spotter."

China waved at him, and he waved back. "Great guy then. He's up for a medal."

Zeke laughed. "All right. Now I get to deliver my famous line."

China glanced at Jake and back. "What famous line?"

"Who ordered pizza?" the men asked in unison.

Chapter 11

Five months later

China inhaled and wrinkled her nose. The hospital smelled like antiseptic.

"You'd think they could do something about the smell these days."

Her complaint caused Jake's chuckle. He leaned over the bed. "If it kills any germs or bugs hanging around, then good."

"I just wish this was over."

"The same way you were with the investigation."

"Yes."

"Something I'm learning about you—that you've got an impatient streak."

"And you don't? I seem to remember you threatening the detective."

"Threatening? Now you're going overboard. I just pushed him to stay on top of things."

"I remember going overboard. Almost drowning."

"But you didn't."

She touched his chest. "Thanks to you."

"No. Thanks to you, he no longer had the gun."

"I don't know what happened. I just knew I couldn't let him have it. We were fighting, and then I was falling overboard. That's all I remember."

"Well, the gun went with you." He picked up a chair and set it next to the bed. "I don't know how I hit him or how he made it back to shore, but there was blood all over my boat."

"The DNA will convict him."

"Yeah." Jake shrugged. "It made it easy to identify him and pick him up. I'd still like to know how he got that bug in your house."

"Me, too."

Jake caught hold of her hand. "Maybe during the trial."

"We're lucky to be alive." She let herself drink in his eyes, his mouth, his chin. She touched his lip.

"Blessed."

"Yes."

A nurse pulled back the curtain. "We'll be taking you back in a couple of minutes."

She glanced up and nodded. "Okay."

The curtain closed, and they were alone again.

China focused on him and bit her lip. She'd wanted to do this for a while, but still the surgery and the recovery left a nervous twinge in her stomach. She pulled her hand free from his and stared at the diamond ring on her finger. When she looked back at him, his grin had widened.

"You like it?"

She tapped his chin with her fist. "I've told you a dozen times I love it. You like my tattoo?"

He laughed. "I've told you a dozen times I love it."

Actually, when she showed it to him, his eyes had teared. The tattoo artist had changed the raven into a rose and put a Scripture around it—"The desert shall rejoice, and blossom as the rose."

God was making everything new.

Even her hair. She liked the short pixie cut the hairdresser had given her. Maybe she'd keep it blond...

Nah. She wouldn't go that far.

Jake rubbed the top of her hand. "Your mom wanted to be in here with you."

"I know. Just like she wanted to come stay after we were rescued. I'm glad I let her then, because it made it easier to say no today." She traced his jaw with her finger. "I wanted you to be here."

He touched the IV in her arm. "You didn't have to do this."

"And go breastless the rest of my life? I don't think so."

He grinned. "Well, I can concur there. Maybe I shouldn't say this, but it feels a lot like Christmas."

"Jake Travis Osborne! That…that's…" She laughed. "Ridiculous."

The curtain opened again. The nurse and an orderly slipped in.

"We're going to wheel her down to surgery now. You can wait in the waiting room, Mr. Osborne, with the others…"

"I will." He leaned over to kiss her and whispered, "I do surgery and sickness, you know. And I do health. I do richer and poorer and lifetime commitment. I'll be waiting."

REVIEWS!

I hope you have enjoyed *Honor Respect Devotion*. It was fun and exciting to write. If you enjoyed it, would you leave a review on Amazon and/or Goodreads? Readers and authors need and love reviews. To review this book, please visit: https://www.amazon.com/Linda-K.-Rodante/e/B012OITZ2Y
Scroll down to this book, click on the reviews already there, and it will give you a place to add your review.

*If you enjoyed this book, please join **Christian Indie Author Readers Group** on Facebook. You will find Christian Books in multiple genres, opportunities to find other Christian Authors and learn about new releases, sales, and free books:*
https://www.facebook.com/groups/291215317668431/

Linda's Books:
Amber Alert, Book 1 of The Dangerous Series
As Long As You Both Shall Live, Book 2
Splashdown, Book 3
Looking for Justice, Book 4
Honor Respect Devotion, Book 5
Pursued, Book 6, Due out Fall 2017

All of Linda's books can be found on Amazon,
https://www.amazon.com/Linda-K.-Rodante/e/B012OITZ2Y

On the next few pages,
you will find a preview of the sixth novel
in the *Dangerous Series.*

Pursued

Christian Contemporary Romance with Suspense

Prologue

Christina Torres ignored the bleep of the man's cell phone even as he did. Although his hand touched its case, his eyes—brown and intense as Cacao Prieto's dark chocolate—never left hers. The fluttering inside caused her to step away, and her back came up against a tree—the tree he'd tied his horse to.

One side of his mouth lifted, and a glimmer of light flicked through the dark eyes. He stepped closer. She tightened her grip on her horse's reins even as heat caught her throat and surged into her face.

Their race across the open field to this stand of oaks had not been their first, but none had left her as breathless as his nearness did today. And that closeness blocked any escape route. Without shoving him and frightening their horses, she was trapped.

A year ago this would not have happened. A year ago she would have shoved him anyway, tried to upset his footing and knock him to the ground. But a year ago, their teasing and competition had everything to do with friendship. When he'd come back from the university this summer, things changed. She knew it from the way her heart trembled each time they were together, the way hummingbirds flitted through her stomach whenever their hands touched, and the way his gaze lingered on her throughout the day.

She thrust aside the thoughts gathering in her head. He couldn't be interested in her that way. The difference in their ages was too great; they'd been friends too long…

But he leaned forward, the half smile giving

way to seriousness, his gaze dropping to her lips. The anticipation of what he would do next cemented her to the spot.

His head lowered, and his mouth settled on hers. Its gentleness sent waves of warmth through her. The hummingbirds spun and flipped and whirled inside. When he pulled away, his smile was gentle, too.

He brushed the long hair back from her shoulder, fingering it, and said in a low voice, "Wow."

The touch of his hand stirred more fluttering inside. His gaze dropped to her mouth again, but after a moment's hesitation, he moved back.

His smile stretched. "Glad you didn't deck me."

She couldn't find her voice. Five years since her dad had left, since her world had fallen apart, and five years since Chase Richards had decided to be her friend. She'd been eleven at the time, and Chase seventeen. He just graduated high school and planned to attend the community college nearby, but he made time for her.

His phone beeped once more, but he made no move to get it.

Her brain searched for a reply to his comment. Being witty was hard when she couldn't think past the emotions surging through her. She cleared her throat. "Maybe I just wanted to see if you were any good."

He barked a laugh. "So I get rated? Who are you comparing me to? Not that pimply-faced Hogan, I hope."

She dropped her eyes, stared at his boots, and swallowed. Her mouth still felt his. She wanted him to kiss her again, but with his arms tight around her, his tall, lean body next to hers.

"Cristina." His hand touched her cheek. "You're beautiful, you know that? But…you're only sixteen. We need to finish this in three years when I've completed my internship." He dropped his hand. "Come on, I'll race you home, and this time I won't let you win."

Her chin rose. She narrowed her eyes. "You didn't let me win. And I'm not beautiful. Don't lie to me." She shoved him aside and mounted the stallion. Anger mingled with the hurt from his words. Why had he kissed her if he was just going to treat her like a child afterward?

She yanked the horse around and dug in her heels. The stallion jumped and stretched its legs. Behind her, Chase shouted something in amused protest; but she ignored the words, leaned over the horse's head, and raced for home.

Chapter 1

10 years later

Cristina straightened the strap of her attaché case and strode down the corridor. The heels of her pumps sounded in the marble hall, the smooth ponytail she'd pulled her long hair into early this morning flipped back and forth.

It would be good to get home and pull the band from her hair, pull on some jeans and drive to the ranch. She could ride hard and fast and let the wind strip the ugliness of this last case from her mind.

"Mizz Torres. Mizz Torres! I'd like to talk to you."

The graveled voice broke through her thoughts, slowed her steps.

"I said I want to talk to you."

She glanced around the hall as she made a turn. One or two other people hurried by. No one looked at her. Where was a guard when you needed them? Her focus settled on the man approaching her. His angry expression hadn't changed throughout the court proceedings. "Yes, Mr. Jordan?"

Five foot-ten inch of gym-sculpted body stepped in front of her. The blue eyes slitted. "You really have no idea what you're doing. You think you got my daughter out of harm's way, but you haven't. That black widow—" he pointed toward the door behind them, "is the one that is abusive. Not me. She sold you a bill of goods, and you swallowed it."

"Mr. Jordan, the court—"

"Don't give me that crap. The court listened to *you*." His look dropped to her feet and rose slowly. "You women do it with your bodies all the time."

She curled her fist against the urge to slap him. The man had showed up at her office a few weeks ago in workout clothes, flexing his muscles, and he'd met her shirtless for a

supervised visit with his daughter. The fact that she hadn't
fallen for something so obvious probably caused more anger
than his concern for his daughter.

"Mr. Jordan, trying to insult me will get you nowhere.
The court has made its decision, and it is final."

"Yeah, well, we'll see about that." He leaned in, the
blue eyes and white teeth flashing. "Nothing better happen to
Leslie. Do you hear me? Nothing!" He whirled, leaving a trail
of musky cologne in his wake.

Cristina took a deep breath and wondered how
someone so handsome could be such a rotter. Well, that went
with the territory, didn't it? As far as she remembered her dad
had been good looking, too.

And Chase. No different. At one time she'd
desperately prayed to see him again; now she hoped she never
would.

Someone nodded at her, and she nodded back, forced a
smile and went past the security check-in. When she pushed
open the heavy door, she breathed in the hot, June air. A ride
today would bring a good sweat and relieve the tension from
the proceedings and Mr. Jordan's attitude.

Chase Richards propped himself against the fence post
and watched Luke Stephens lean forward and lift the stallion's
foot. When the man had invited him out back to finish their
conversation, he had no idea the horse would still be here, nor
in such obvious good shape. Cristina's stallion. Probably
seventeen or eighteen years old now. Horses lived longer these
days, just like people; but still, seeing Max's tough beauty
again jolted something inside him.

Stephens lifted a hoof pick from the wooden shelf
attached to the fence post and began to dig dirt and dung from
the horse's hoof. He didn't look at Chase. "So, you're saying
you knew Cristina when her mom owned this place?"

Chase nodded, not sure if the man's surly attitude was
part of his nature or personal. He'd seemed friendly enough
until Chase began to explain about Cristina. The driving force
that had compelled Chase to come had not lessened on his trip
here, from Virginia to Tennessee. No one had ever won an

argument with God, anyway. So, why had he tried? He'd known this would be humbling and hard. Not that that was an excuse, but he hadn't counted on the town, or this place or this horse stirring memories he'd buried years ago.

He'd made a mess of things back then, and for quite some time now, he'd dealt with God's urging—no, more like demand—to make things right. After this long, he'd questioned? Cristina either would care less, think him crazy or wouldn't want to see him at all. Most likely, the latter.

He shoved the thoughts away and moved forward. "Yeah, we use to ride together a lot."

Stephens glanced up then dropped the stallion's front right foot and reached for the back one. "Give me a little room, will you? I don't want him lashing out and hitting you."

Chase moved to the front of the horse. Where were his brains? He knew that. You didn't stand behind a horse. Cristina had taught him better than that.

The man rested the stallion's knee on his own, digging the pick into the bottom of the hoof again. Dirt flew. The boots and broad-brimmed Stetson the man wore marked him as cowboy, but the subtle nuances in his speech and tone told Chase there must be something more. Still, Chase wouldn't mind a broad-brimmed hat right about now. And although the mountains in the distance stood blue-gray against an aqua sky, the late afternoon sun had inched the temps close to ninety.

"So, you've come back to Tennessee to see Cris. Does she know you're here?"

"No, I thought a…surprise…might work better."

The man stood and eyed him. An uncomfortable minute passed. "Does she want to see you?"

Well, Stephens had caught that hesitation quick enough and pinned it just as quick. Not short on intelligence, that was for sure.

Chase better come clean. "Probably not. I left at a bad time in my life and hers—without a word to her. I want to make that right."

The man's brow lifted. He nodded and waited.

Chase examined him again. Stephens had said earlier that he'd bought the house and the ranch from Cristina's mom, but Chase knew that before he came. He'd done his research. It was why he'd come to the ranch. Walking in on Cristina at work was not what he wanted. Meeting her somewhere else, somewhere neutral, would be better. He'd thought about the ranch, so he drove out here.

The man had said something about "we" when talking about the ranch. Chase assumed he meant his wife and himself. What if...

"You're not married to her, are you?" Silly question and off-putting in the way he'd said it. Why didn't he want to think about Cristina being married? At twenty-six, she probably was. He hadn't found anyone with whom he wanted to spend his life, but that didn't mean she hadn't. His internet search had shown no name change; but, as a lawyer, maybe she'd kept her maiden name.

Stephens walked to the left side of the horse, traced his hand down Max's leg and lifted the hoof. The man had a sturdy solid build. Something Cristina would have appreciated.

"Make a difference if I was?"

Chase shrugged. "No. Like I said earlier, I haven't seen her for years, but I need to speak to her." That's all it was—God leading him to make the situation right. Another situation right.

Stephens bent and scraped the bottom of the hoof clean before lowering it the ground, then moved to the left back leg. "I'm not fond of surprises, and Cris might not be either. I'll let her know you stopped by, though. How can she get in touch with you?"

Which didn't answer Chase's question. Avoided it, in fact. Disappointment dropped into his stomach, but he shoved it away. His infatuation with the girl ten years ago meant nothing. After this, they would both go their separate ways. An apology and back to Virginia and the opioid study he was involved in.

Behind him, the creek of a door caused him to swing around. A woman emerged from the house. The roof's shadow across the deck and long walkway partially obscured his view. Long, dark hair like Cristina used to have caused his muscles to tighten. The woman came down the ramp from the house, a hand on her rounded mid-section. Pregnant, his mind filled in, and at the same time, the knowledge that this wasn't Cristina.

LINDA K. RODANTE   148

His muscles relaxed.

When she drew closer, the woman nodded at him then touched Stephens' arm. "Don't put Max away yet. Cris is coming over to ride."

Chase smiled at the woman. So this was the man's wife. Good. And this could be the perfect opportunity to talk with Cristina, get this over with and get out of here. He glanced at Stephens. His jaw tightened. He dropped the horse's leg.

The woman's gaze bounced between them, quick to pick up on her husband's tension. "I'm sorry. Is something wrong?"

"No." Stephens' voice held an unwavering tone.

Chase slid a palm down the stallion's nose. "Doesn't need to be. If I could wait here until she arrives—"

"No."

"I've come a long way—"

"You said it's been a decade since you've seen her. It can wait a little longer."

Chase eyed the man. The first time he'd gone white water rafting, they'd sat waiting on their rafts for someone to open the Ocoee River's dam, waiting for the waters to flood out, waiting so they could go bucking and swirling over the rocks and racing downstream. The frustration of the wait had let him know he had an impatient streak. That same impatience filled him now.

"All I want to do is talk with her. I could just stop down the road and flag her down as she comes this way."

Stephens straightened, pulled a smart phone from the holder on his belt and began to text.

"No, stop."

The other man's gaze rose, green eyes boring into Chase's dark ones.

Chase swallowed the impatience. What was the man's problem, anyway? Why so protective? Did Chase look like some kind of nut? "Not like that. If you have to tell her I'm here, do it in person."

"I'll do that, but you need to leave."

"I'm not trying to hurt her, you know. I'm just trying to put something right."

"We'll let her decide if she wants you to do that." His gaze moved to the woman beside him. "Alexis, this is Chase Richards. He's come to see Cris. Chase, this is my wife, Alexis. You can give her your number, but we'll let Cristina decide if she wants to see you. I'll put Max in the corral and walk you to your car."

Cristina leaned over the stallion's head, giving him her signal to fly. He flew, and she laughed. She'd ripped the elastic band from her hair right after mounting, and the feel of the wind in it and on her face tore the vestiges of the long day from her mind. If she could just stay in this moment.

The unique combination of scents, horse and leather, made her as hopeful as the wine she'd started drinking not long after Chase vanished. But she'd given that up as soon as she realized it could create a problem. The degree she wanted would demand her best effort, so, she'd dropped the wine glass and picked up her books. And nothing bad had happened to Chase. His family's attitude told her that. They were sorry about the situation but silent. Obviously, Chase wanted nothing to do with her—not after his father died.

She closed her eyes and swallowed. Stop it, woman! What has gotten into you? You're past that, over it and him. It's been years, and you're no longer that gullible teenager.

She straightened and pulled back on the reins. "Easy, Maximus, easy." Her hand dropped and patted his neck as he slowed. The combination of Chase's desertion, her mom's death, and being forced to sell Max and the ranch had kept her away from here for years. Even though Luke Stephens, the buyer, had said she could come ride anytime, there was too much pain in the memories.

She eased back on the reins. The meeting with Alexis, another lawyer, a couple of months ago had proved valuable in more ways than one. She and Alexis had a similar heart for abused children and the meeting on the county's drug problems had put them on the sale committee. Learning that she was Luke's wife had opened the door to a visit to the ranch after years of being away.

"You've got to come ride Max again," Alexis had

encouraged her, and Cristina went that weekend. She'd come every week since.

The stallion slowed to a smooth canter. Perspiration beaded on Cristina's forehead and back, but the dappled sunlight on the path and the emerald and jade of the trees eased the stress across her shoulders.

She smiled thinking of Jianna's reaction in the courthouse parking lot right before she headed out. "Where you going, girlfriend? Want company?"

"I'm headed to the ranch. Going horseback riding. Want to come?"

Her partner's mouth dropped open like a baby bird's. "Are you out of your mind? A horse? Me?"

She grinned, knowing Jianna's aversion to animals and all things country. "Yep. It would do you good."

Jianna snorted. "Horse hair, dirt and poop. Not in my life."

"Well, it's back in mine."

"What life you referring to, girlfriend? These last few years all you've done is work, eat and jog—by yourself. Your social life is the same s a rattlesnake's. Nonexistent."

Cristina rolled her eyes. "Well, you wouldn't classify this as social, either, but—"

"No handsome hunk out there to show you the ropes?"

"Don't need it or him. Sure you don't want to come?"

"Like you'd catch me riding something with no gas pedal and no brake." She slid a dark hand through a head of unruly, black hair.

"You'd love it."

"Not me. But if you do want company, Judge Carson seems to have an eye out for you lately."

Cristina couldn't stop her scowl. "That man needs a wife. Oh, yeah, I forgot. He has one."

Jianna laughed. "Well, if you find a couple of hot men while you're riding, then call me."

"Hot men don't interest me. You know that. I'm into nice and trustworthy. Someone who keeps his word and sticks around no matter what."

"Yeah, I hear ya. But can't you have both?"

Cristina shook her head. The hope that there were a

few good men in the world rested in the same marginal area as her belief in God. If God was real as she'd once thought, and if he still cared…

She stopped at home long enough to change before heading to the Stephens' place. The Stephens' place… She sighed. Well, it was now. And Luke and Alexis kept good care of it. She was thankful for that. She might have sold it to someone who would let it go to seed or not keep up the house. Instead, Luke seemed to have kept up with everything and added to it.

When she arrived, she slipped around back as usual. Seeing Max saddled and ready for her, she breathed a thank you under her breath and took the horse out through the gate.

After a run over the field, she reined Max right and entered the cover of a large stand of trees. Luke had left the fifteen acres wooded with some nice riding paths. Across the road was government land, acres more where she could ride for hours if she wanted.

She sighed. No wonder Chase was on her mind. Being back at the ranch and riding in places she remembered brought those years back vividly.

The heat beat the smell of pine from fallen needles, but the shade fell across the paths with welcomed relief. She straightened in the saddle, putting her shoulders back, relaxing her legs, closing her eyes…

Max jumped. Her head snapped back, and her fists tightened on the reins. The stallion gave a half buck before charging forward. Cristina shoved her feet against the stirrups. The crack that reverberated in her ears was followed by another.

"Max!" She yelled, trying to hold on. One foot slipped all the way through the stirrup, and she pressed it hard against the stallion's side to catch her balance. Another crack sounded. Max charged around the bend in the path.

If she fell, her foot caught like this… She wrestled it free and tried to right herself just as Max leapt a branch in the path. She flew from the saddle and plummeted to the ground. Pain tore through her head.

Author Biography

Linda was born and raised in Florida. She must have a gene for the love of reading because she remembers reading whatever she could get her hands on at a very early age. At twelve, she wrote her first story only to have it thrown away by her friend's father! At fourteen, her own father bought her a typewriter, which she used until computers made correcting mistakes easy. ☺

Linda worked as a Center Director for the Pregnancy Center of Pinellas County, and for eight years, she was a speaker with the Tampa Bay area's Community Campaign Against Human Trafficking (now called FREE). Her blog, *Writing for God, Fighting Human Trafficking*, can be found at https://lindarodante.wordpress.com/. Her author blog is at http://lindarodante.com/ . She's also on Twitter and Facebook.

After growing up and raising a family in Florida, Linda and her husband now live in Tennessee. They have two grown sons and three grandchildren. Her mother was a missionary to Israel and Indonesia.

Linda's books have won finalist and semifinalist awards with the American Christian Fiction Writers Genesis and First Impressions Contests. She hopes her writing reflects her love of God and is an encouragement to readers.

Her romantic suspense series can be found on Amazon. http://amzn.to/1Uo6I0a.

Made in the USA
Monee, IL
11 January 2023

25094568R00085